# The Quilt

# The Quilt

Pensacola Wilson

★★★★★

HOLLYWOOD BOOKS INTERNATIONAL

Hollywood • Los Angeles
2008

Published by Hollywood Books International
7095-1240 Hollywood Boulevard
Hollywood, California 90028-8903
http://www.americanpopularculture.com



Publisher's Note
This is a work of fiction, a product of the author's imagination. Any relation to actual character, place, incident, or any other matter is purely coincidental.

Library of Congress Cataloging-in-Publication Data

Wilson, Pensacola.
The quilt / Pensacola Wilson.
p. cm.
ISBN 978-0-9789041-2-8
1. Bay Saint Louis (Miss.)--Fiction. 2. Poor women--Fiction. 3. Domestic fiction. I. Title.
PS3623.I58567Q85 2008
813'.6--dc22
2008033367

## One

Bay St. Louis slept in the afternoon sun. Grass curled up in lazy s's as daffodils hung their dozing, yellow heads. Too hot to fly, seagulls bobbed on the grey gulf waves which had last touched shores in Key West and now gently nudged the Mississippi coast as if to wake it from its nap. Even the azaleas, screaming pink in the morning, had pulled their petals back from the sharp sunlight and taken refuge in the cool green of their leaves. The oaks, their arms stretching out to embrace the neighborhood, sighed and slowed their breathing to the slightest rustle and stir. Only the magnolias laughed, their deep, waxy leaves and open creamy blossoms, wide and frothy, a stark contrast to the quiet stillness of an August heat.

The sand here was no match for the powdery fine whiteness of the sand in Destin or Pensacola, but it was still much whiter, much finer than the same on more western beaches. Further from the shore, between the straggles of grass, stretched great dusty patches of packed dirt. The combination of sand and sun in soil deterred the hearty green in the yards of more northern neighbors. Although this dearth was not the fault of drought. Even now great cumulus clouds gathered on the horizon, rolling toward the curving shore.

But in this array of curve and motion, the gulf waterline stood on the distant horizon, flat and straight as the edge of a pastor's collar or a wall, flush and plumb. Highway 90, more often called Beach Road by the locals, ran parallel to the water and was intersected by Dogwood Pass, which cut north away from the beach. The streets on either side of Dogwood were stately and paved. Grand Southern homes bowed to business dinner guests and curtsied to luncheon ladies. The houses on Dogwood, on the other hand, were small and rundown, once the servants' quarters for the homes that now turned their backs on property long cut off by wrought iron gates, ten foot hedges, or stone walls that kept secrets and blocked eyesores.

Dogwood was really just an alley. No powerful citizen ever lived here to argue in front of the city council that this road really must be paved. That light brown dirt, packed down and laced with sand, only made way for bare feet and bicycle tires and the occasional lost tourist or turtle. Orphan dandelion patches broke the edges of the street, ragged and worn. No clean curb or concrete sidewalk was ever poured on this back way. Those were saved for the major thoroughfares on either side of Dogwood. Peachtree Lane to the east and Hargrove Court to the west.

Peachtree harbored the old Southern manors, pastels with gracefully curving white pillars, balconies, and porches all around. Traces of Greek revival – and the plantations that were inspired by such – influenced every cornice, path, and window frame. Dirt was shipped in through the Mississippi River delta to replace the sand-laced dust so prevalent on Dogwood and not so conducive to the extravagant grass and haughty rose bushes desired for their rich greens and spoiled pinks.

Hargrove, on the other hand, harbored the newer styles. Traces of Frank Lloyd Wright, exposed stone work, lower-leaner lines, and natural earth tones erased the porches, pillars, pastels, and white trim of the more traditional homes. Rose bushes were replaced with decorative grasses with exotic names like Ogon and Variegatus.

Between Peachtree and Hargrove, though, ran quiet Dogwood Pass where stood the humble home of Eudora Renfroe and her calico cat, Betty Grable.

Although Dogwood wasn't paved, the dirt was packed in a north-south sort of sweep that set it apart from Eudora's front yard. Every afternoon, she got her rake out of the closet next to the front door and walked out to the road. There she placed her rake along the edge of her yard and pulled it back toward her front porch where Betty Grable sat and watched, occasionally licking her front paws. If Eudora couldn't afford grass, she would make sure her dirt was raked.

When she was done with the first pass, she picked up the rake and walked back to the road, matched her placement next to the first mark, and pulled her rake toward the porch again. She continued this process until she had made perfect parallel lines running across her yard. Sometimes a small patch of grass or a dandelion cluster popped up. Eudora raked over these like they weren't even there, refusing to let any obstacle alter her perfect lines.

After ten passes, Eudora stopped and leaned on her rake to rest. On this particular August afternoon, the thermostat read 102 degrees and the air hung heavy with 85 percent humidity. She knew that to be true because she had bought a yellow plastic weather station at pennySMART, which hung from the eve on her porch, and she glanced at it every time she passed by. In fact, for the two weeks that she had owned it, she had checked it hourly. She believed that instrument like she believed the word of God as recorded in her Bible, the NIV. Eudora wasn't sure why she had become so obsessed with weather here in her old age. It seemed to her to represent something of the cycles of life, a certain cosmic rhythm of sun, then clouds, then storm.

Eudora turned to the shore. Her house was five up, but through the trees, if she stood at a 45 degree angle to her front porch and looked southwest, she could see a narrow sliver of sand and ocean and horizon and sky and Beach Road. She had fallen into this habit after her fiancé Frank had enlisted during World War II. For years, she had watched that sliver of road every day waiting for him to come home and marry her just like he had promised.

Eudora looked at the straight line of the water on the horizon then she looked down at the straight rake lines in her yard. Straight, she smiled, she had always liked straight. In fact, that's probably what she missed most about Frank. Straight lines.

Frank had been the janitor at City Hall. Five days a week, he walked north on Dogwood – he lived just two doors down from her – turned left on Main Street, pulled out the ring of seventy-three keys he had hooked on his belt loop, unlocked the door of City Hall, and went to the janitor's closet. The first thing he did was get the feather duster and make a pass over every single surface in the offices and hallways. Then he went to the closet and pulled out the industrial broom. The pole a two-inch diameter leading to a thick wooden plank with boar bristles shooting down about three feet wide…

Suddenly, a gust ripped through. Eudora turned around and glared at the willow tree in Bernice Holloway's yard. The broad branches hung over the chain link fence that separated their properties. Every time the wind blew, the fronds shed like fur from a mangy dog. Eudora hated those fronds in her yard, disturbing her perfect rake lines, and today, she decided, was the day to do something about it. She threw down the rake with certain purpose, marched around the chain link fence, charged up the slipshaw wooden steps of her neighbor's house, and banged on the door.

"Bernice," she hollered. "Bernice Holloway come out here right now."

"Go away," she heard Bernice holler from behind the peeling door.

"Answer this door right now, Bernice Holloway, or I'll bang your garbage cans at 6am." If there was one thing Eudora knew, Bernice could not abide mornings.

Frank had loved mornings and Eudora had looked forward to the day he would come back and they would get married and they would wake up early and do morning errands together. Make breakfast. Sweep the house. Cook Toad-in-the-Hole. For years, Eudora had asked herself why he hadn't come back for her. She was too poor for a phone, but he never even wrote. She had waited for so long. And that Bernice, trotting all around town with her sailor. Showing off her wedding plans and then the wedding pictures for more than a year. She hated that Bernice Holloway. And she was glad when Bernice's husband had dropped dead of a heart attack at only forty-three. And she didn't care who knew it.

"I mean it Bernice. You promised me you'd cut back this tree weeks ago."

Bernice didn't answer this time, so Eudora rattled the knob. The door was locked.

"That's it. I'm calling the city on you," Eudora screeched as she turned and stomped down the porch stairs. She was furious. Those Holloways always were good-for-nothings. Rubbing weddings in your face. Dropping leaves all over your yard. Well, the fire department had ordinances and fines and Eudora knew their number.

She marched around the chain link fence and stomped up the stairs of her own porch, the shaking and shuddering of such a sort that it knocked her mailbox askew. It was the old-fashioned, Southern type of mailbox. A flat, metal box that hung on her house just left of her front door. Betty Grable tried to muster some enthusiasm for the activity, but she could only manage a yawn as she curled up in a patch of sunlight.

"Ugh," Eudora grunted, disgusted with the disorder of the universe. She studied the uneven mailbox, pushed the high side down, stepped back to check that it was even, and went inside to call the Bay St. Louis Fire Department to settle this matter once and for all.

Eudora went in her house and slammed the door behind her. Not a moment later, she heard the scrape of metal on wood and knew the mailbox had slipped again. She looked up at the heavens and shook her head. What had she done to deserve this injustice? Willow leaves in her yard and now a perennially crooked mailbox. The phone call to the Bay St. Louis Fire Department would just have to wait. She had bigger fish to fry.

Eudora opened her front door, stepped out onto her front porch, and inspected the offending mailbox, again pushing the high side down. When she did it this time though, it slipped right back down and something fell out from behind that rusty old box and fluttered to the ground. Eudora peered down at it and pondered whether it might be worth the considerable effort it would take her tired old body to bend down and pick it up. After all, she'd just gotten through raking. She leaned over and squinted her eyes to get a better view of the object. Betty Grable merely waved her tail in the air and continued to doze in the August sun.

The object appeared to be a small envelope. About four inches wide and three inches tall. Dry and yellowed and dimpled. The back side was facing up and Eudora could see that the V of the flap had aged a more brownish shade of yellow than the rest of the paper.

After a moment's reflection, she decided it might be worth the effort and bent the rest of the way to pick up the envelope. Once she had grunted her way through the retrieval, she straightened slowly and turned the envelope over. What she saw next pierced her heart as if someone had stabbed it with one of her metallic red knitting needles. There written in an old familiar handwriting was her name and address. Why she'd know that scribble anywhere.

Just then Eudora heard Bernice's front door slam. Eudora watched her neighbor striding across her yard, up around the chain link fence, and back down to the porch where Eudora was standing. Bernice wore her orange zinnia housedress and had her hair up in pink sponge rollers. Eudora hated it when her neighbor went out of the house dressed like so, but she barely noticed in her current state of shock.

"Miss Eudora Renfroe," Bernice started, "don't you dare call the Bay St. Louis Fire Department on me. You know darn well I can't afford that fine. The Royce boy said he would do it. It's not my fault he's in two-a-days for fall football. He can't do it til Sunday."

Already pale and white haired, somehow Eudora had gone even paler. Bernice looked at her, blinked, and changed her tone altogether.

"Good Lord, Eudora," Bernice said, "what happened to you? You look like a turkey on Christmas Day. A few stray willow leaves can't be all that bad."

Eudora staggered toward her porch rocker. When the backs of her legs hit the seat edge, she collapsed back into the chair. Bernice walked up the steps.

"What is it?" Bernice asked. "What's wrong?"

Eudora held the letter in front of her, her hand trembling. Bernice took it. She turned it over and read the address. Then she looked at the return address.

"Uhhh," Bernice sucked in. "Well, I'll be. It's from Frank."

Bernice looked at Eudora. It would be difficult to say which one was more shocked. Bernice's dark brown eyes bulged wide while Eudora's grey eyes sunk back even deeper into their watery caves. After the two had stared at one another for several moments, Eudora made a waving motion toward Bernice who understood she was to open the letter and read it.

Bernice turned the letter over looking for the best point of entry. The paper was brittle and weathered. She worried that it might crumble in her hands. She decided to slip her pinky nail under the flap on the back and found that the old glue gave way quite easily.

Slowly, Bernice slipped the letter out. Folded in half, the paper crackled like the driest winter oak leaf as she unfolded it.

"My dearest Eudora," Bernice read aloud. "I am in Atlanta. Take the bus on Friday. We have an appointment at City Hall first thing on Monday. I love you and can't wait to call you Mrs. Frank Andrews."

As Bernice read, Eudora rocked in her chair. My, but she rocked and rocked. She rocked forward and back. Faster and faster. She rocked and rocked and rocked. She rocked back to when she was eighteen with chestnut hair and bright eyes and pink pouty lips. She rocked away the wrinkles and the liver spots and the arthritis. She rocked and rocked. She rocked back to the exact moment when Frank had left for the war. Then she rocked through all the years of missing him. The years of anguish. The years of worry and wonder. The years of "old maid" whispered behind her back. She rocked and rocked and rocked. A letter lost for years. Wedged between the mailbox and the wall. Her marriage. Her children. Her life. Ripped from her by a careless mailman. By the cruel hand of fate. It was not to be borne, Eudora decided. It simply was not to be borne.

She stomped her feet down to stop the rocking. Then she stood, snatched the letter from Bernice, and crumpled it in her fists. The fragile paper turned to dust, and Eudora wiped her palms together to be rid of it. The dust floated to the ground and much of it disappeared through the porch slats.

"What are you doing?" Bernice gasped.

Eudora brushed past her nearly knocking her down. "I'm calling the Bay St. Louis Fire Department, Bernice Holloway. I'm sick of you and your damn willow tree," Eudora snarled, passing through the door and slamming it behind her.

The old rusty mailbox, only hanging by one nail now, swung from the force of the door. Slowly, that last nail gave way and the mailbox clattered to the ground. Finally startled into action, Betty Grable jumped up and dove off the porch. As she tore through the front yard, Bernice couldn't help but notice that the cat destroyed nearly every one of Eudora's hard earned rake lines, once perfectly even and perfectly straight.

## Eudora's Tips and Tricks
## for Quilter's Daily

### #58

Now don't you sass me. I Sewanee. There is no way, no how, I'm gonna wash my swatches or my quilt before competition. Do not charge up to me in the fabric section of pennySMART and challenge me on this. The next one of you dear readers who does so might just have to eat a knuckle sandwich. I don't care what kind of concoction you try to put in the water. Fabric is never the same after it's been washed. The competition quilter needs the crisp bright color and clean snap of unwashed fabric. Wash before you sew? Fiddle-faddle. You're making me cranky. But, as usual…

Happy Quilting!

The Bay Press

# Comedy Corner

As ya'll know, we're continuing our series "Things you won't ever hear a Southerner say." Thanks for your submissions, keep 'em comin'. We'll publish the top five every week. We're pokin' fun at ourselves folks, so let 'er rip! Stereotype AWAY!

Here's this week's winners:

1. Gimme some unsweet tea, please.
2. Who's Elvis?
3. Where can I buy a gun control bumper sticker?
4. I'll take pine nuts and bean sprouts on my salad.
5. Duct tape can't fix that.

14

# Two

Eudora closed the door behind her and leaned back against the roughened wooden planks. The show of anger she had made had taken the last bit of her strength and she now wilted like a picked daisy in the sun. Slowly, her knees gave way until she looked like little more than a crumpled, soiled t-shirt tossed in the general direction of the laundry basket. Lying there on the floor.

After several moments, she tipped forward onto her hands and knees and crawled toward the phone. Knee hand knee hand. Then she stopped because she realized she wasn't breathing. In out in out. Just breathe. She had had surgery – a radical hysterectomy for a faulty ovary. She had broken her pinky toe chasing after Betty Grable when the cat had brought a dead mouse into her bedroom. And she had once fallen off the roof of Bernice's house onto the pile of pine straw they had just pushed off during a spring cleaning. She had been black and blue, bruised all over. But she had never felt pain like this.

She stopped and looked at her fingertips. They tingled but they were numb at the same time. She poked her index fingers with her thumbnails – she couldn't really feel anything. She stuck her right pinky in her mouth and chewed on it. Nothing. Wait. She had stopped breathing again. In out in out. She went back on her hands and knees and continued toward the phone.

Eudora's house was a two room shotgun. One square in front, one square in back. A tiny hallway in between with a bathroom on the left and a kitchenette on the right. The front room, as she called it, contained a green plaid couch with oak arm rests and a dining table, but Eudora hadn't seen the table in over thirty years – at least not for more than an hour – the time between the finishing of the last quilt and the placement of the backing for the next. For the past two years, she hadn't seen the table at all. That's the amount of time she had spent on this last quilt. The pinnacle of her sewing career. A king size masterpiece. 5000 pieces. Hand stitched. The tiniest pieces of fabric in an intricate garden scene.

She didn't want to do a garden scene. In fact, this commission had violated all her sacred beliefs as a quilter. Diamonds. Circles. Squares. She was a loyalist to the traditional Southern patterns. But when Allison Gordon had called with an offer of thousands for a fairy garden, Eudora couldn't say no. For someone who hadn't bought a new dress in twenty years (thrift store only) or eaten anything but canned goods for thirty, this was a fortune.

As she crawled past the table, she paused to look at her quilt, which hung almost to the ground. She picked up a corner and examined it closely. Tiny stitch after tiny stitch, evenly spaced, perfect. Then she saw it. She pulled her breath in sharply, stood and rushed to her glasses, resting on an aluminum TV tray. She shoved them on her face, grabbed the same corner of the quilt, and examined it again. There it was. She had not imagined it. A glaring hole. A missed stitch.

Eudora crossed to her sewing box, a great green plastic square in the corner. She opened it and pulled out her seam ripper. Now she had already gone three more feet in the same sweeping direction. To rip this out was to lose a day's work at least, but Eudora was far too proud of her work to let a quilt go out with a skipped stitch.

She sat down at the table and slipped the tiny knife edge of the ripper under the first stitch and pulled up cutting the fine thread. Then she proceeded to the next stitch and the next. Cutting the thread and pulling the loose part through. Careful not to enlarge the hole the needle had left or to damage the fabric in any way.

Methodically and slow, she held the quilt four inches from her nose and squinted through her six dollar pennySMART glasses. Inch by inch the hours went by until she was startled out of her trance by her telephone.

Eudora laid the ripper down on the quilt then carefully folded the edge up and over the table. By the fifth ring, she finally made it to the phone, cream and plastic and hanging on the wall.

"Eudora?" she heard as she put the phone to her ear.

"Yes, Allison, who else would it be?"

"For goodness sake," Allison said, "what took you so long to get to the phone? That house can't be more than four inches square."

Eudora had learned better than to get into a fight with a commission, so she held her tongue and asked, "Why are you calling, Allison?"

"My mother's in town and she can't come back for Christmas when I'm giving Suzy the quilt, so I was wondering if we could come by and see it right now?"

"You know I never let anyone see a quilt before it's done," Eudora began.

But Allison interrupted, "I knew you'd understand," and hung up.

Eudora's insides felt like a washcloth wrung tight. She was still six inches from the missed stitch. At the slow rate she was going, taking special care not to widen any holes, she was at least thirty minutes away from the offending portion. She felt a little woozy and leaned against the wall. All she knew was this: she never would have gotten up this morning if she had any idea it was going to be such a bad day.

# Eudora's Tip and Tricks
## for Quilter's Daily

### #59

Okay ladies, now hear this. I bought one of those vinyl tablecloths at pennySMART and tacked it up on the wall next to my sewing machine. I could lay my fabric out to test my patterns and it stuck with nary a pin. You should try it. A better design wall you'll never find. I Sewanee. As always…

Happy Quilting!

# Three

Allison Gordon lived in one of those mint green and white confections on Peachtree. Truly, her house looked like it might be sitting on a bakery shelf, the dahlias in the garden like so many multi-colored sprinkles.

Eudora knew it would only take Allison five minutes to get here if she cut through the backyard. She had her mother with her, so that might slow her down a bit. Seven minutes, if Eudora was lucky.

She rushed to the stove and put on a kettle of water. Then she crossed to the quilt, picked up the ripper, and tore the stitches out with abandon. Tucking the quilt up under her arm, she carried it to the kettle, which was just starting to steam, and she held the quilt above it running her thumbnail over the holes. She examined them closely. Not bad. Maybe they wouldn't notice. She folded the quilt on the table with the ripped out stitching face down.

Eudora sighed and glanced at the clock. Two minutes. She had two minutes to spare. Then she looked out the window and received a cruel shock. Eudora simply could not believe what she saw.

There, on the ground, lay her rake and the unmistakable mark of Betty Grable having run through the front yard. Eudora hustled out the front door, picked up the rake, and began pulling it from the road back to her porch with the energy of one half her age. The cat had only disturbed about three passes worth, and, despite arthritis, humidity, and considerable heat, old Eudora was able to patch her straight lines in less than three minutes. "Thank goodness," she muttered, "they're runnin' late." Just as she lumbered through the front door and tucked the rake in the closet, she heard the dreaded knock.

"Eudora? It's me," Allison called out, "and I have my mother with me."

Eudora took a deep breath, smoothed her hair, then her dress, and opened the door.

"Welcome, welcome, do come in," she sung out, stepping back to make way for the ladies.

"I don't believe you've met my mother, Pylis," Allison said.

Just as Eudora nodded and was about to offer the ladies iced tea, Pylis shrieked and rushed to the table. She snatched up the neatly folded quilt and shook it out. When she did, the bottom fell on the floor. Eudora hurried to the tail and picked it up. To think, her precious creation, brushing the floor.

"Allison had told me you were talented," Pylis began, "but I had no idea. The detail. The colors."

Eudora wasn't one for blushing or stammering, but she was very proud of her quilting and grinned broadly. She had twice been named Gulf Coast Quilter of the Year. Last time, she had finished second place in the National Quilt-Off. In fact, she planned to enter this quilt in just that event. She had hand picked every piece of fabric for color, texture, and pattern. She had hand cut each piece to create this free form garden scene while preserving a classic circle pattern throughout the background. Her stitches had reached the pinnacle of patience and precision, so tiny, so uniform.

"Yes, I know. It is quite good, isn't it?" she boasted.

Allison slid her hand under the center of the quilt and examined a particularly graceful iris. "I told you, Mom. Eudora's work is world class." Turning to Eudora, Allison added, "I'll give you a bonus if you can get it to me by the end of the month. I wanted it for Christmas, but I'd love to give it to Suzy for her birthday."

Eudora looked at her calendar. Then she looked down at the quilt, slightly adjusting her hold to hide the ripped stitching in a fold. It was the first week in August. The new timeline would give her only three weeks to finish the bottom quarter of the quilt. Eudora began to shake her head, "it's not possible. It's just not possible," she said.

"Mrs. Newman and Mrs. Warr will be there. If they see this, you'll be sure to get more commissions," Pylis urged.

"I don't like to drop names," Allison added, "but Mrs. Taylor and Mrs. James Reynolds will be there too. Suzy's birthday party is a society event. I have to have this quilt there."

"It's just not possible," Eudora said again.

"I'll double the bonus," Pylis said.

Eudora hesitated. The money they were offering. It was beyond belief. She felt a rush of adrenaline. But she wanted to enter this quilt in the national contest...

As if Allison could read her mind, the young mother added, "If you get it to me by Suzy's birthday, you can have it back for the contest. Just get it back to me by Christmas."

Eudora continued to stare down at the quilt. This would mean twenty hours of work a day. No raking, no fighting with Bernice, no time to mourn Frank...

"Okay," Eudora said, looking up at Pylis, then turning to Allison, "I'll do it."

"Ahh!" Allison screeched and hugged Eudora just before bolting out the front door. No doubt, she was rushing to begin her party planning in order to show off the quilt to its prime advantage. Such a coup as this, possibly the greatest quilt ever made, should affirm her place, Allison must have thought, on the Gulfport Country Club Charity Event Planning Committee. And what honor could be greater than that?

Unfortunately, the hug jolted Eudora and she dropped her strategic fold. Pylis looked down and saw the ripped out stitching. She and Eudora looked up. Their eyes met.

"I won't tell her," Pylis said after a long pause, "but make sure to fix it so we won't see needle holes."

Eudora had never been so insulted in all her life. As if…as if…

She pulled herself together and smiled. "Of course, I would do nothing less."

Pylis dropped her end of the quilt on the table and patted Eudora on the wrist. "I know, dear. I know," she said.

Oh, the condescension. Eudora's fake smile became faker, her lips thin and stretched.

After Pylis left, Eudora walked to her closet and pulled out her scrap basket. If this were going to be a world class quilt, the kind of quilt that would set the Gulfport Country Club Charity Planning Committee on fire, Eudora would need texture. The surprising juxtaposition of velvet, corduroy, seersucker, linen, satin, against a grainy silk. Cotton, wool, muslin, against a somber tweed. Indeed, she may even throw in the most surprising twist of all – an ordinary knit.

She began to scheme and plan. This would be a quilt that would win great prizes, fetch an enormous price, and bring her fame. With this quilt, she would secure an endless stream of commissions from the ladies in pastel homes. Perhaps she would even get orders from the ladies in the Wright houses – albeit quilts with cleaner lines and more neutral shades, say varying tones of beige. Nevertheless, she would find herself in the most elite of homes measuring the beds of children, grandchildren, guest rooms, and even the bed of the mistress of the house. For so long, she had struggled to make ends meet. A single woman, poor and ugly. The old maid abandoned, left even *before* the promised altar. And now. And now, she would have the opportunity to pick her name up out of the garbage dump, polish it up, and place it on the trophy shelf. Oh, how Bernice would hate that. Eudora slowly smiled.

She put the scrap basket on the couch and sat down next to it. Sinking her finger into the cuts of cloth, she closed her eyes and smiled. Here, a brocade, there a crepe, her fingers caressed the threads reading every woven strand as if it were a Braille poem by Whitman himself. This was the language she spoke. This was the language she understood.

When she closed her eyes, she could see sheep grazing on green slopes in Montana. She could see the shearers. Then those spinning the wool into thread. She could see the cotton grown in Georgia, plucked by hand. She could even see the chemist in a lab developing the latest spandex, lycra, polyester. Eudora was not an elitist in this regard. She could appreciate the natural and the man made fiber and the fabrics that were woven from a combination of them both. Oh, she had friends who would only stitch in cotton. For them, the natural, soft cloth with its ability to take such a nice shade when color dyed – this was the only true cloth of the veteran quilter. But Eudora had more progressive sensibilities when it came to material. And she knew that the exploitation of these sensibilities – the understanding of the ways in which she should use these fabrics – the ways in which she could be revolutionary with these scraps – this prowess would distinguish her from the legions of other quilters and secure her place in quilting bee legend.

Eudora heard a banging at the door. She snapped, "Go away." Bernice turned the knob and walked in, Betty Grable weaving through her legs and over to the water bowl.

"How'd you know it wasn't them?" Bernice asked.

"I knew it was you."

"How'd you know?"

"Cause you're the nosiest woman south of the Mason-Dixon line, and I knew you couldn't help yourself more than about two minutes to come over here and find out what they wanted."

"Well?" Bernice asked.

"Well what?" Eudora shot back.

"Don't make me ask you."

"I won't,"

"Eudora, you are the most irritating woman."

"If that's not the pot calling the kettle black."

Bernice came over and sat on the couch, the basket of swatches between them. She reached in and pulled out a moss colored piece of moleskin. She rubbed it on her cheek. "So soft," she said.

Bernice snatched it from her hand. "Don't put your old, greasy face on that. Go away. Take those

26

darn curlers out of your hair. I don't know who you're curling your hair for anyway. Where you going?"

"I'm playing Bunco at Patsy's tonight. I'd invite you, but you're too mean. Ever since that time you made fun of Patsy's wig, the ladies just haven't wanted to see your face."

"I bet she sees to it she's got that thing on straight now."

"It's true. She does. Now what'd they want?"

"They want it faster, as always."

"More money?"

"Mind your own business," Eudora snorted.

Bernice's eyes lit up like fireflies. "How much more? Enough for grass? I sure would like to plant our yards for once. Can you just see it? The grass all green and soft in your toes?"

"Fiddle-faddle. I don't have time for grass or your nonsense. Now get. I Sewanee."

"All right. I'll go," Bernice said while standing up. "You sure you're okay?"

"Course I'm okay, why wouldn't I be? They're harmless enough."

"I mean about the Frank thing."

"What? Please. That was years ago. Makes no difference now," Eudora said ducking her head deep into the swatch basket.

"Okay, well, if you need anything."

"All I need is for you to scat."

Bernice moved to the door and put her hand on the doorknob. Then she paused and looked back at Eudora. "Oh, I almost forgot to tell you. There's a tropical depression in the gulf. They say it's heading into Texas. Don't you have family there?"

"Never mind my family," Eudora grunted. "Now get on outta here. If I wanted to watch the weather, I'd a gotten this TV fixed fifteen years ago when it went out."

"You know, I've been meaning to ask you," Bernice said. "Why don't you throw it out seeing as it doesn't even work? Why you holding onto it?"

"It's too heavy to move," Eudora said.

"I could get the Royce boy to come get it on Sunday when he comes over to do the tree," Bernice offered.

"Go home," Eudora retorted.

"Suit yourself," Bernice said, shrugging her shoulders and closing the door behind her.

Eudora counted a few seconds to make sure Bernice was really gone. Then she pulled her head out of the swatch basket and peeked out the window. She saw the flap of Bernice's orange zinnia housedress as she turned the corner of the chain link fence.

Eudora reached for the moss moleskin, still on top and wiped under her eyes and blew her nose in it. Then she looked over at the TV. The TV balanced out the room. It acted as a counterbalance to the heavy couch. To take the TV would be to leave a blank white wall. When Eudora sat down on the couch, she didn't want to stare at a blank white wall, for heaven's sake. Now surely Bernice could understand a simple thing like that, couldn't she? Balance. Form. And another thing, Eudora had no more family left. Texas or anywhere. Everyone had died off. Good Lord. Did Bernice ever pay one lick of attention to anything but herself? Texas indeed. Fiddle-faddle.

Eudora's Tips and Tricks
For Quilter's Daily

## #60

You know those leftover scraps of batting? Well ladies, don't you dare throw them away.  I mean it. Batting picks up better than any swifter or whatever they call it. Swipe your work area after you're done and you'll catch up every little thread and fabric snippet. Safety pin it around your sponge mop – your floors have never looked so good. As always…

Happy Quilting!

# Four

Eudora calmly decided there was nothing left to do but to kill herself. There was no question in her mind. This was what she must do. Of course, she wasn't thinking about the quilt at the moment. She was thinking of Frank.

She looked around the beach and realized there really wasn't anything to help her here. Even if she walked out to the end of the dock and jumped, she would find herself in water about two feet deep. Bay St. Louis had shallow surf. You had to wade out for a mile to find the first drop off. No, if she were going to kill herself, she would need something more dramatic.

She thought about jumping off her roof. But it was only about ten feet off the ground. All she would end up doing would be to break some bones and live in misery in the hospital for two months. Peeing in a catheter. She fell off Bernice's roof into a pile of pine straw and only got bruises. No. She would have to commit to more extreme measures.

She thought about walking north up Dogwood from the beach. In her imagination, she passed Bernice's house then her own as she continued up to Main Street. To jump out in front of a car speeding on Main Street: this was her plan. There was always a local late to bridge club or a teenager taking a chance, laughing with friends, not paying attention. Or maybe she'd get really lucky and get there just in time for a drunk tourist from L.A. flying by at seventy miles an hour. Now that would do the trick. A drunk tourist from L.A. Seventy miles an hour. Yes indeedy.

But Eudora didn't move. She just continued standing in the middle of the great stretch of white sand that was the Bay St. Louis beach. She looked down at her feet completely buried and wiggled her toes so she could see them as the granules fell away. Her toenails glowed a pale yellow in the afternoon sun. Dead cuticles speckled and framed them in a dry whiteness. Purple veins broke through the skin's surface on the top of her feet. Ugly. Ugly and old. These feet disgusted her. She burrowed them back in the sand. Perhaps they were best left unseen.

Then Eudora looked out over the water. It was choppy, gray, turbulent. She giggled to herself. She suddenly remembered hearing her daddy say, "You see that clear, ol' water in Florida? It's full of nothin' but seaweed. You see that ol' muddy water in Mississippi? Full a fish, crab, oysters. You know what the moral of the story is? Lotta lovin' goin' on in the mud!" She laughed out loud. That was a good one. He was a character, that's for sure. She sure did miss him.

Then she became still and quiet again. She turned around and looked at Beach Road, running parallel to the water. Nobody knew how long she had stared out at that road. The nervous stomach. The restless nights. She had hoped so hard that it actually strained her heart. Still now, she could feel it straining and twisting in her chest. She'd like to step in front of a car on Beach Road. It would bring her a certain sense of dramatic irony or poetic justice or something, but no one ever drove fast enough here. This was a leisurely road for beach gazing. No, she would have to make it up to Main Street. That's where she would find some business traffic. Even the tourists were in a hurry on Main Street. So she turned and walked up Dogwood Pass kicking a beer bottle cap with her bare feet. Then she made it to Main and took a left. What a mess she was. Her silver hair high and wild. Her dingy, olive green, polyester dress stuck to her thighs. No bra. No undergarments at all. Just jostling along. Barefoot. No makeup. Crazy old Eudora.

When she found herself across the street from City Hall, she stopped. She turned and faced it. She looked left. Then right. She need only wait for a speeding sedan. That would solve all her problems.

She waited, stared at City Hall, chewed on the thumbnail of her right hand. Then she saw it. Actually, she heard it first. The straining engine, the squealing tires. She knew it was coming. Her sedan. The sound of a racing car coming closer and closer.

This was her moment. Her answer to a universe untidy and unfair.

But as the sound came near to her, out of nowhere, Betty Grable appeared, and with a wave of her tail, she walked out into the middle of the street and sat down. Eudora was bewildered. She didn't know what to do. What was this nonsense? Was Betty going to steal her thunder? Ruin her plan? She, Eudora, was supposed to be splattered in the middle of Main Street, make all the papers the next morning. Not Betty Grable. Most definitely not.

The sound came nearer still. Eudora whistled, clapped, snapped, called to her cat. *Here kitty, kitty, kitty.* But Betty merely found a sunny patch on the road, stretched out, and began licking one of her front paws, her tail waving to a silent beat.

Eudora looked toward the approaching sound. She could now see the car, a white sedan speeding toward her. Was Betty really going to lie there and let the car hit her? This was crazy. Eudora had no idea she had such a crazy cat.

Closer and closer. The car was speeding toward them. Eudora whistled, clapped, begged. But it was no use. Betty looked at her and yawned. Then she rolled over and stretched out in the sun.

For a split second, it occurred to Eudora that perhaps this wasn't such a bad thing. After all, if she were dead, who would take care of the cat? Bernice couldn't be trusted. One time she brushed her teeth with glue. A real space cadet. But if Eudora and the cat died simultaneously, problem solved. Perhaps Betty already understood this and was sacrificing herself on the street like those ladies in India who throw themselves on their husband's funeral pyre.

Eudora glanced up at the car speeding toward them, looked at Betty Grable stretched out on the street, glanced back up at the car, dove for the cat, grabbed her, and scrambled to the other side of the road just as the sedan whizzed past.

"Oh, fiddle-faddle," Eudora snorted at Betty. "You ruined my big chance." Betty just jumped down and ran after a lizard darting under a bush.

"You're welcome!" Eudora called out after her. "Ungrateful rat." But Betty Grable was now long gone.

As Eudora brushed herself off, she looked at the steps leading up into City Hall. She turned, walked up the steps, and strolled into the front door like a little girl walking into a doll store for the first time. Her eyes wide as Texas. Looking all around. In years and years she had never stepped foot in City Hall. Not since Frank had left for war. The décor looked the same. The worn gray wall-to-wall carpet, the faded blue curtains, the water fountain silver and bulky and square. The water fountain…

Why she remembered that water fountain. It looked exactly the same. But it couldn't be the same one. No water fountain could continue operating for that long. But what a resemblance. Eudora walked to the fountain, bent over, and took a sip. Yep, the same lousy water. Warm and metallic. It's a wonder she had lived through it the first time. She hadn't oughta drink too much from it now.

She stood and turned and there he was, Frank, meeting her for lunch.

He walks down the hall so young and fresh. Brylcreem slicking his hair into a dark wave and shine worthy of Rudolph Valentino himself.

"Hey doll," he says as he leans in to kiss her. He is carrying a basket.

"Whatcha got there?" she asks.

"Picnic lunch," he answers. He takes her hand and leads her out the back door where they walk for awhile through dogwood trees and azalea bushes until they come to a clearing with a carpet of lush green grass. In the center, under the shade of a magnolia tree stands a picnic table. Frank leads her to it, brushes off the bench, and offers her a seat.

"Why thank you, Frank," Eudora says, "You're awful sweet to feed me. Seems like I always got too much month left at the end of all my money."

# Eudora's Tips and Tricks
## For Quilter's Daily

## #61

No matter how experienced we are, we all get a needle prick from time to time. When (not if) you do, soak your fingertip in rubbing alcohol. Girls, you will be amazed the next day. Your finger won't hurt one bit. You won't even see the hole. As always…

Happy Quilting!

The Bayou Press

## Local Fisherman Really Reels 'Em In

Jimmy Tucker of Bay St. Louis – but then all ya'll know the Tuckers! – beat out fishermen from all over who came to the Jordan River for the 10th Annual Speckled Trout Fishing Rodeo. In three days, he managed to pile up thirty-five pounds of trout for the Grand Prize, an all expense paid visit for two to Michael's Steam House up the river. Michael's is also Jimmy's sponsor. You've probably seen him in their red t-shirts and caps. (Come on, Michael, time to spring for a red satin jacket. And then again when are you gonna spring for a Little League team?)

"This is a humungous honor," says Jimmy. "I want to thank God and my family for always being there for me and making me the best fisherman I am. I am very glad to carry on this rodeo tradition from my dad, and I hope to teach it to my son."

Congratulations, Jimmy Boy, we at The Bayou Press (Cairo and me) are really, really proud of you. We knew you could do it since you caught that catfish when you were still only six years old.

## Five

"Eudora Renfroe! Please tell me it's not true," Bernice shrieked, charging into her neighbor's bedroom.

Eudora groaned, rolled over, and pulled her covers over her head.

"It's not true."

Bernice jerked the covers down.

"I will not have people saying I live next door to the crazy cat lady. Tell me it's not true."

"It's not true," Eudora repeated, reaching for the covers.

Bernice snatched them away again.

"Don't you humor me, Miss Smarty Pants. I doubt you even know of what I speak."

"Go away," Eudora growled.

"I most certainly will not, not until you tell me it's not true."

"It's not true."

"I've worked very hard to keep up my reputation in this town. I don't want people thinking

I'm crazy just because you are. Birds of a feather flock together and all that."

Betty Grable jumped up on the bed and curled up beside Eudora in moral support.

"Get out of my bedroom, Bernice, or I'll poop your stoop."

"Ugh! I knew it. I knew it. I knew that was you all along. And you had the nerve to blame it on the Royce boys."

Eudora picked up a coaster and threw it at Bernice hitting her on the chest. Betty Grable meowed as a sort of cheer as Eudora extended her index and middle finger.

"V for victory," Eudora said. "Two points."

"Well, I never," Bernice huffed, crossing her arms. "And why in the world are you sleeping in your glasses."

"So I can see my dreams," Eudora said as she picked up a box of tissues and tossed it at Bernice's head, tagging her right between the eyes.

"Two more points," Eudora shouted. "That's four. I win. Now get out!"

"Josh Singleton said he saw you laughing and talking and walking with an imaginary person out behind City Hall yesterday. I want to know if that's true. Are you crazy?"

"Get out," Eudora reached for her lamp.

Bernice hurried toward the doorway.

"If you throw that lamp at me, I'll never speak to you again," Bernice said.

"Hallelujah! Now I'm throwing it for sure. You shouldn't make it so appealing," Eudora said as

Bernice disappeared. A few moments later, Eudora heard the front door slam and she put the lamp down.

"We showed her, didn't we?" Eudora whispered to Betty Grable who ducked her head for a behind-the-ears scratching.

Bernice stomped down Eudora's stairs and shuffled her feet through the yard disturbing the rake lines as best she could. Dissatisfied with the job she had done, Bernice walked to her house and got her blower. She kept it around for the Royce boy. Honestly, it was a little too heavy for her to handle. But her anger gave her superhuman strength and she was able to hold it up long enough to blow it up into the willow tree knocking just enough fronds into Eudora's yard to make a decent mess.

Eudora heard the engine roar and knew exactly what Bernice was up to. This wasn't the first time Bernice had intentionally blown fronds into the yard. Eudora got up, put on her robe, and shuffled to the side window. As she pulled back the curtain, Betty Grable leapt onto the ledge. Eudora looked at her cat and snickered.

"We'll show her, won't we?" Eudora said.

She walked to her kitchen, opened her utensil drawer, and took out tongs. She then pulled a bowl out of a cabinet and crossed to the kitty litter where she lifted out the largest and plumpest of Betty Grable's doodles.

Eudora then went to the sink and held each pebble under the water to rinse off the kitty litter, returning each freshened turd to the bowl.

She then peered out the window just in time to see Bernice set the blower down and walk back into her house. Perfect timing.

Eudora opened the back door then looked left and right to check for witnesses. No one. Betty Grable skirted past her and disappeared through the bushes.

Eudora tiptoed to Bernice's back stoop and dumped the present on the welcome mat. Slowly, quietly, she crept back to her house to sit and wait, a noiseless, patient spider.

Not a moment after she closed her door, she heard a screech from Bernice's house.

"Mission accomplished," Eudora smiled and shuffled back to bed.

## Eudora's Tips and Tricks
## For Quilter's Daily

### #66

Okay girls, many of you, like me, have cats and those cats love to curl up on our quilts and nap, don't they? The problem is – how do we get all that cat hair off the quilt? Vacuums don't quite do the job now, do they? The solution? Buy dishwashing gloves from pennySMART with crosshatching on the palms. Run your hands along the quilt and the fur will come right up in balls. As always…

Happy Quilting!

The Bayou Press

## Singleton, Martin to Wed September 26th

Mr. and Mrs. Joshua Singleton of Bay St. Louis are pleased to announce the engagement of their daughter Annie Singleton to Billy Martin of Biloxi.

The bride-elect is the granddaughter of Mr. and Mrs. Avery Rose and Mr. and Mrs. Harvey Singleton. She is a graduate of Bay High School and is currently attending the Kenshaw Bible College. She hopes to head the women's ministry at a Gulf Coast church.

The prospective groom is the son of Mr. and Mrs. Bob Martin Jr. and Mr. and Mrs. Frank Perry. He is the grandson of Mr. and Mrs. Bob Martin Sr. and Mr. and Mrs. Billy Barker. He is a graduate of Biloxi High School where he studied body shop. He works at Allen & Sons on Main.

The couple will exchange vows September 28th at First Baptist in Bay St. Louis.

# Six

Eudora could not believe what she was hearing. Dull thuds against her back door. She knew exactly what that sound was: Bernice was throwing the cat poop at her door.

"Now you cut that out," Eudora bellowed, barely daring to pull back the curtain and peek through the back door window.

Bernice pitched a turd right at Eudora's face. It splattered and slid down the glass leaving a trail of brown sludge behind it.

"Those were my favorite slippers," Bernice shouted. "pennySMART doesn't carry them anymore. They're irreplaceable."

"Stop being so dramatic," Eudora snorted. "Just throw them in the wash."

"I will not sully my washer with such, such crap." Bernice hurdled another turd at the glass.

Eudora didn't even flinch.

"Why, Bernice, I can't believe you just used such a profane word. And you, a Christian woman."

Bernice hurdled her last pebble then broke down in tears.

"You see what you've done to me?" she asked.

"What's that?" Eudora asked.

"You've turned me into a potty mouth."

"You should be thanking me," Eudora said, dropping the curtain. "Give you a little spine. Although I'm surprised you're worried about a little cat crap in your washer, your house being such a pig sty."

"Pig sty? Thanking you? Well, I never," Bernice huffed.

"I think that might be the first thing you ever cleaned up. Why not take all that hateful energy and put it toward cleaning your house?"

Eudora heard nothing but an indignant little screech as she walked over to her sewing table. She giggled under her breath. She knew exactly how to stick it to Bernice.

Eudora leaned over her quilt and examined it carefully. No one would ever expect green velvet in a quilt, so green velvet it would be.

She sat down and threaded her needle. Then she began the tiny, uniform stitching that was the hallmark of her legendary pieces. She knew no one who had her perseverance and patience. Tiny stitch after tiny stitch, she would get lost in the rhythm, like her heartbeat, or her blood pulsing through her veins.

She stitched the rest of the day and deep into the night until Betty Grable started rubbing her legs and purring. The cool night air had begun to stiffen Eudora's fingers. Feeding the cat would bring a welcome rest.

She stood and walked to the refrigerator.

"Yes, beloved, I know exactly what you want."

She took a small piece of folded foil out and put it on the counter. Betty Grable purred loudly and rubbed back and forth against Eudora's leg.

Eudora unwrapped the catfish and cut it into tiny pieces. She then bent down to retrieve her cat's bowl from the corner, poured some dry food in, then stirred in the fish.

When she placed the bowl back down on the floor, Betty Grable dove for it, gobbling the soft fish up right away. She licked the dry kibble, ate a few bites, then lost interest.

"Such a snoot," Eudora smiled. "Just like my Frank."

"Did I hear somebody talking about me? My ears are burning." Frank asks, grinning as he walks around the corner.

Eudora crosses to him and pecks him on the cheek.

"I declare," she says. "Where have you been?"

"I have to make a living, don't I?"

"You mean to tell me you've been at work all this time?"

"Which hand?" he asks.

For the first time, she notices he is holding his hands behind his back.

"This one," she says, pointing to his left hand.

He smiles and brings a bouquet of daisies out from behind his back.

"How do you always know?" he asks.

"I don't know. Just psychotic, I guess."

That sets them into the giggles for a good two minutes.

"What do you want for dinner?" Eudora asks.

"Gumbo, doll."

"Gumbo it is," she says, moving toward the kitchen.

Frank walks over to the quilt, slips on his glasses, and bends over to examine it closely.

"You got a lot done today. Your stitching is impeccable. You should feel really proud. You don't charge enough considering the amount of time and labor you put into this work."

"Amen," she laughs. Then pauses, "Why did you dance with Bernice at the crawfish festival last night?"

"Just being neighborly. Making her feel included. You jealous?"

"I was sipping a hurricane waiting for you to ask me. Then I looked up and saw you dancing with Bernice. Just surprised me, that's all."

"I thought it was important for your friends to like me, to be close to your friends. Why are we having this conversation?"

"When I was twelve, I found a snake in the garden. I tiny snake – a short, sweet snake. I brought it inside and put it in a goldfish bowl, no water, just a turquoise castle, some palm trees, and pink boulders. I loved that snake. I fed it bugs and worms. And one day I wanted to show it off to Bernice and I stuck my hand in that goldfish bowl to take it over to show to her and it bit my thumb. I was so afraid that the bite might be poisonous that I ran to the kitchen and pulled out a knife to cut off the tip that snake had bitten. Now I have just one question for you – why did you bite my thumb?"

Frank walks over to Bernice who sits at her quilting table. He takes her two hands in his. He examines her fingers and finds the one unnaturally shortened on her left hand. He leans over and kisses it.

"I don't know what that snake was thinking. These are the sweetest little fingers in the world."

But Eudora is in no mood for romantic condescension.

"Fiddle-faddle," she says as she stands and walks away.

## Eudora's Tips and Tricks
## For Quilter's Daily

## #69

Quiltaholics, listen up. Stop throwing away those toilet paper rolls. Use them to wrap your scraps around. You won't have to re-iron and you'll never have to dig through a scraps box again. I just started doing it and I love it. Just line them up in a drawer according to color. (Oh, that's another tip, keep a dresser drawers in your sewing room for all your material.) As always…

Happy Quilting!

# Bernice's Quick Recipes
## for Busy Quilters

## #1

Ladies, I finally talked the editor into letting me do a column too. My neighbor does the quilting tips. Now I'm gonna do the cooking tips. Don't worry. I know you're busy cutting those tiny triangles and squares. Making all those little tiny stitches. I'll give you quick but yummy ideas so you can feed your hubby and your tikes and get right back to the sewing room. Here's the first one:

### Sausage Balls

½ pound sausage (I like the spicy kind)
1 cup shredded cheddar
1 cup baking mix (like when you make pancakes, they won't let me use brand names)
1 tablespoon chopped onion (I use the

purple one because it's real sweet)
½ teaspoon salt
½ teaspoon pepper

Turn your oven on real hot. About 420°. Mix all your stuff up then roll up one-inch balls. Put them on an ungreased cookie sheet (you'll get plenty of grease from the sausage). Then bake for about fifteen minutes. Makes about eighteen balls. If you have a hungry family, you might want to double the recipe.

Have You Some Good Eatin'!

The Bayou Press

## *Member* at The Little Theatre

Come on down, folks, for the immortal classic from the South's own Carson McCullers. *The Member of the Wedding* will be playin' at the Bay St. Louis Little Theatre on Friday and Saturday night at 8pm. Of special interest to ya'll might be Marcy's daughter as Frankie Addams.  Come on down and support Tammy, won't ya'll? Neighborhood favorite Addie Jenkins will be playin' Berenice Sadie Brown. Proceeds go to Little League. See ya'll there!

# Seven

"I hope you don't mind me just stopping by," Allison said nonchalantly as she passed the quilt, lifted up a corner, and examined it closely.

"May I get you a glass of sweet tea?" Eudora said, crossing to the refrigerator.

"Don't mind if I do," Allison sang out.

"So what brings you over to see me today?" Eudora asked.

"I just wanted to check on your progress. I've been bragging about your quilt down at the country club, and I wanted to make sure you're on schedule."

Eudora poured a glass of tea.

"I'm ahead of schedule, as you can see," she said.

Allison dropped the corner and took the glass of tea as Eudora handed it to her.

"I've been meaning to ask you," Allison started.

Eudora crossed her arms slowly.

"Why didn't you ever marry?" Allison asked.

Eudora narrowed her eyes.

"The quilt is on schedule. I'll have it ready by your daughter's birthday if I have time to work on it. Without interruption," Eudora replied.

A knock at her door. Eudora looked up to see Pylis walking in.

"There you are. I thought you might be here," Pylis said to Allison.

"Yes, you started worrying me with all your doubts about Eudora and the quilt. I thought I better stop by."

"Doubts?" Eudora said, raising her right eyebrow and turning to Pylis.

"I just didn't want my daughter to be made a fool of. She's been bragging up this quilt all over town. And if you don't finish, she'll lose face."

"And why wouldn't I finish?" Eudora asked.

"The stitching...," Pylis began.

Eudora grew dark and glowered at Pylis who coughed nervously and looked down at the floor.

"And..." Eudora waited.

"And," Pylis paused, "it's just that you're so..."

"So...," Eudora waited.

"So old. There I said it. It's no secret. You must be at least eighty. I mean you could die or lose your eyesight."

"Out," Eudora bellowed.

"Out?" Allison asked, bewildered.

"I appreciate this commission. I truly do. But if you or your mother step foot in here one more time, I'll throw this quilt on top of a bonfire in my backyard just as sure as I'm standing here."

"Uhh," Allison gasped. "Come on, Mother. Let's go."

"You're fired. We don't want your dern quilt anyway," Pylis shouted.

"Shh. Mother. Stop. Eudora, don't listen to her. You won't hear another word from us. I swear." Allison grabbed her mother's arm and dragged her to the door.

"She'll never burn that quilt. She's put too much work into it," Pylis said.

"Shh. Mother. Eudora, don't listen to her. We're sorry we bothered you."

Allison dragged her mother out the door as Eudora slammed it behind them.

Betty Grable trotted in the room and wound her way through Eudora's legs. The old woman wobbled, grabbed for a chair back, and missed. Before she knew it, she had lost her balance and was falling. As she went down, Eudora's head hit the corner of the table and by the time her head bounced on the wooden slats of her floor she had already blacked out.

Eudora's Tips and Tricks
For Quilter's Daily

#70

Seems like some folks think I'm old. Fiddle-faddle. But I will admit that sometimes I have trouble seeing which side of fabric is "up" especially when sewin' at night, and especially when the piece is a solid white or something like that. So cut your piece in the morning light, girls, and put a little piece of tape on the "front." Remember! I solve all your problems! (And I just cannot believe the editorship of this magazine honestly believes there is any room on these pages for recipes.) As always...

Happy Quilting!

# Eight

Bernice Holloway charged across her backyard and up to Eudora's back door with her copy of *Quilter's Daily* rolled up in her fist. She banged on the door with the magazine, "Eudora, you open up this door right this minute. I'll break your window. Don't think I won't."

Bernice paused and heard nothing.

"I don't know where you get off bashing my recipes to the readership. The editors quite rightly decided that my recipes were important for busy quilters on a deadline. You of all people should be able to appreciate that. I do declare. I'd like to be able to say the older you get the meaner. But to tell you the truth, you've always been mean as mosquitoes. Eudora! Don't you ignore me."

Bernice paused again. Still nothing.

"When I got engaged, you spread all those rumors we were already spending the night together. Me and him. Well, what of it? Why was it any of your business? A polite neighbor would just turn the other way. But no. Not you. And when he died, you were downright gleeful. Oh, don't deny it now. You were so happy for me to be lonely just like you. You're hateful, Eudora. That's right. Downright hateful."

Bernice paused again.

"Eudora? Eudora?"

Bernice put her hand on the knob, turned it, and slowly pushed in the back door.

"Eudora?"

Betty Grable meowed and dashed out between Bernice's legs. Bernice jumped with a start and held her heart.

"Goodness, but you scared the dickens out of me. I don't know what Eudora sees in you."

Betty Grable turned and looked at Bernice – tail high in the air, waving slightly.

"Shoo. Git. Now git," Bernice said.

Betty Grable hissed, then turned and disappeared into an azalea bush.

Bernice stepped gingerly into the bedroom then through the middle hallway to the front room.

"Eudora? Eudora? Well. I guess I can expect a lamp flying at my head any minute now, but I'm coming in. You're scaring me. You're not one to be so quiet."

Bernice heard a groan and looked toward the sound. There she found Eudora lying on the floor.

Bernice rushed over and knelt beside her neighbor. Eudora's eyes snapped open and she tried to stab Bernice in the leg with a knitting needle. Bernice was able to dodge the attack, receiving only a grazing scratch.

"Ahh," Bernice screeched. "What's wrong with you?"

"Get out of my house," Eudora growled.

"You're injured. You need help."

"Don't make me tell you twice."

"Where in God's name did you get a knitting needle in your state? And that strength?"

Eudora swung the knitting needle all the way back to the floor opposite where Bernice was kneeling. Then she started a low growl and whipped the needle again toward Bernice who fell to the right to avoid it.

The needle sunk into a floorboard. Eudora tugged at it, but it wouldn't budge. She finally let go and threw herself back, spread eagle on the floor.

"Have you about worn yourself out?" Bernice asked.

Eudora narrowed her eyes and looked at her neighbor.

Bernice moved to help Eudora up. "Well, come on then. Let's get you to bed."


When Eudora woke up, she heard the quiet rustle of a turning page. She rolled over to see Bernice sitting in the bed beside her reading the first edition of Flannery O'Connor's *Wise Blood*.

"I beg your pardon," Eudora said.

"Glad to see you're conscious. Was worried about a concussion," Bernice said.

"Get out of my bed," Eudora snarled.

"What are you worried about? If I was going to make a pass at you, it would have been back when you had a figure. I can tell you that for sure."

Eudora snatched the book from Bernice. "Give me that. You're gonna break it. It's rare. A collector's item."

Bernice reached out and felt Eudora's forehead. She knocked Bernice's hand away.

"Well, okay then. I can see you're fine. Just a bump on the head. I'll just take my leave."

"Commercial fishing licenses just went on sale," Eudora called after her.

"Hurricane's coming," Bernice called over her shoulder as she left.

The Bayou Press

## Commercial Fishing License on Sale Now

The Mississippi Department of Marine Resources just let us know they'll be selling licenses April first, good for the next year until May 1st. If ya'll wanna compete at the bass rodeo in July and you plan on catchin' more than fifty pounds of fish, you gotta have a commercial license. So get on down to Bayview and register with Boyd. He told me yesterday only Jimbo and Dougg had been down, so ya'll wake up and git down to see Mary Alice.

# Bernice's Quick Recipes
# for Busy Quilters

## #2

Ladies, I disagree with the person who shall not be named and her hateful comments in the last edition. She's a busy body and never could mind her own business. Always callin' the fire department on a body or tattle-tale gossipin' in the neighborhood. You know the type. Anyway, if there's one thing I know, it's what a quilter needs. Ya'll are busy, and I know that. I can get you fed, and fed good. So don't you mind her. She's a fool and you know it (who ever heard of not washing your pieces before sewin' them in). I never. Well, anyway, here's this week's recipe.

Chicken Pot Pie

1 tablespoon vegetable oil
¾ cup chopped up onion

3 cups of chopped up chicken meat
Couple dashes all-purpose flour
Pinch of salt
Pinch of pepper
One shake white onion powder
One shake seasoned salt (if you like it a little spiced up, add some of that T.C. – you know what I'm talking about)
Tiny pinch of garlic powder
¼ cup frozen corn kernels
¼ cup frozen cut up carrots
1 cut up celery stalk
3 cut up red potatoes
1 cup chicken broth
9-inch store bought pie crust

Preheat oven to 425.

Heat oil in sauce pan. Add onion and sauté. Add chicken and keep sauté-ing. Sprinkle all the spices on the chicken. Don't forget to keep on stirrin'! Then add corn, carrots, celery, taters, chicken broth. (You may want to cheat the broth by adding a cube of bullion for more flavor.) Bring mixture to a boil. Add dashes of flour til thickened like you like it.

Pour stuff in pie crust. Put top of pie crust on top and pinch around the edges to seal the crust to the dish. (If you wanna be fancy, you can brush the top with beat up egg.) Poke a fork through the top. Then put the whole thing in the oven and bake 8 to 10 minutes, until crust is golden brown. Mmm-mmm, delish.

Have You Some Good Eatin'!

# Nine

The water swept over her head, not blue, not gray, but green, the green of the Gulf. It whipped her around and pulled her down. Not once did she fight it. She just went limp and let the water urge her arm up and around, her leg back, her chin to the side. Eudora actually liked the movement. It made her feel wrapped and warm and supported. No more back pain. What arches?

The water surged and pushed her to the surface. She took a breath of air just before she was tugged to the sandy bottom. Her knees skimming. Nicked by a shell. The slightest discomfort and sting. But she was never afraid. She knew how to ride the rip tide. She understood the rhythm of the waves.

What she didn't understand was the salt water up her nose. Try as she might to blow it out. Or hold her nose during the particularly rougher surges, she just couldn't keep that salt water from trying to strangulate her. Let's be honest. That's what it was trying to do, right? Well, suffocate, anyway.

Frank wraps his arm around her waist and swims upward. When their heads break the surface, she pushes him away.

"I don't need a prince. I'm doing just fine," she snaps, snorting salt water out of her nose.

"There's a hurricane coming. You have to get out of the water."

"I've lived here for eternity. No hurricane's got me yet, and I rode out Camille."

"Why are you so hard headed?"

"Fiddle-faddle. You're the hard-headed one. Now git. I'm fine."

Frank swims toward shore, a freestyle stroke, long, lean, and strong.

Eudora watches after him then turns her face to the sun. She lies back and floats on top of the water. Her dress billowing all around her.

The next wave up, curving and crashing down on her. And then she was under again turning and twisting in the will of the tide. The upper water tugging her shoulders and head toward shore. The lower water tugging her legs out to sea. Weightless. Powerless. Eudora tumbled to and fro in the current, comfortable and free.

A dolphin circled her, nudging her before swimming away. A school of tiny silver fish flitted around her, tickling her skin. She saw a manta ray and a jellyfish, but still she was never afraid. Instead she closed her eyes and smiled, convinced she could smell her mother's cornbread.

Then the rip tide changed moods. It became red, angry like a bee sting. It drug Eudora to the floor of the ocean, slamming her knee down into the sand. She knew she had skinned it by the stinging sensation the salt water produced. Next, she was twisted and her arm scraped against the raw, rugged edge of that broken shells jutting from the sea floor. This time the cuts screamed, a fierce incisions. She began to fight the tide. Thrashing, screaming…

When she awoke, two men were strapping her to a gurney. She looked up and saw Bernice, arms folded, lip pursed, glaring down at her.

Bernice leaned into Eudora when she saw her eyes snap open, "I knew you wouldn't like it. But you've been out of it for hours. Tossing. Turning. Calling out for Frank. Pushing him away. You should see your sheets. Tied up in knots. You fell and bumped your head. I thought you were okay, but I think you've got a serious injury. A concussion or something."

"I'll get you for this," Eudora snarled. Then turning to the paramedics, "You think I'm sick. You should go see her house. She has orange soda cans actually stuck to the counter. She has gum ground into the shag carpet in her bedroom. Go look. You won't believe what a slob she is. Bacteria growing everywhere. You should get the penicillin concession for that place. Be wealthy men."

"People all over town been telling me about your crazy spells. Mary Alice. Addie Jenkins. Beau Wade. They say you talking to imaginary people. Babbling on," Bernice said. "Just let a doctor look you over. Check you out. You should see your eyeballs. Red as the gladiolas outside my kitchen window."

"Gladiolas are funeral flowers," Eudora said.

The paramedics rolled Eudora out to the ambulance.

"I'll show you red," Eudora continued. "Come close. I'll slap you silly. Then you'll know red. Everywhere you look'll be red. Blood in your eye."

Bernice followed after her and stood at the rear door of the ambulance as they pushed Eudora in.

"You'll thank me for this some day," Bernice said.

"I'll murder you for this someday," Eudora growled as the paramedics closed the doors and the ambulance pulled away.

# Ten

Eudora picked up a green pee and threw it at the hospital door. It bounced off and rolled across the linoleum toward her bed. She picked up another pee and threw it at the door again.

In the hallway, she could hear Bernice, "Well, where is she? Room 212. She's not in here. Or you said 213. Okay. Okay. I'm going. Out of my way."

Eudora heard the rattle of metal instruments crashing against carts and trays. She picked up another pee and threw it at the door. She knew if she timed it just right she could hit Bernice smack on the forehead as she walked in the room.

She gauged Bernice's height on the hospital door. Eudora threw another pee. Bingo. That would be her forehead. Actually, now that she thought about it, it might just be her chin. Eudora picked up another pee, gauged Bernice's forehead and threw it. The pee bounced off the door, hit the floor, and rolled to the cluster of pees puddled by the bed. Now that would definitely have been her forehead.

Bernice bellowed, "Why I don't know why it has to be so confusing. Just point me to her room. And I want a blanket and a cot rolled in there. I'm staying. Visiting hours don't count for me. Why I've been her neighbor for I don't know how long. We was girls together. And then she was in my wedding. We're practically sisters. You know that. Why you wanna bother me with this nonsense? Paperwork at a time like this. I never. Now move on outta my way. I'm gonna see her and not you or anybody's gonna stop me."

Eudora picked up another pee and cocked her hand back over her shoulder. Waiting for her prey.

The door opened. She threw the pee. And it hit *Allison* square in the cheek.

"What? What are you doing?" Allison sputtered, rubbing her face.

"Sorry," Eudora started, "I was aiming for your forehead. Actually, somebody else's forehead."

Allison walked to the bed, "Who in the world throws green pees? I'm telling you, you're losing it. Who you wanna throw pees at?" She sorted through the pees with her index finger, picked one up off Eudora's tray, examined it, popped it in her mouth.

"It's a long story. A really long story," Eudora sighed.

"I packed up my family to head north for the hurricane and I heard you were in here. What's wrong? Are you gonna be able to finish the quilt in time?"

"What's wrong with *me*? What's wrong with *you*?" Eudora asked. "I'm lying in a hospital bed and you're worried about your damn quilt?"

"I'm just saying."

"You get on outta here. I promised you the quilt and you'll have it. I already warned you once not to bother me with this nonsense."

Allison started toward the door, then paused and looked back at Eudora, "One more thing. Should I take it with me? The quilt, I mean. I don't want it to get damaged in the hurricane. I mean. I'm just saying."

"So you'd leave me here, like a dog, but for God's sake you'd take the quilt."

"It's not that. It's just..." Allison petered out.

"I can take care of the quilt. I can take care of myself. Now you get on outta here and take care of your family," Eudora said quietly.

"Okay. We're staying in Jackson. You can call my at momma's house if you need me," Allison walked quickly to Eudora, kissed her on the forehead, and left.

Pylis peeked her head in quickly, "Sure we can't take the quilt?"

Eudora picked up a pee and threw it at Pylis. It hit her on the top of her head and stuck in her bee hive of a hairdo.

Pylis ducked back out of the room and Eudora could hear her say, "She threw a pee at me. It's stuck in my hair. Get it out of my hair. What is wrong with that woman? She's plum crazy. Why don't you snatch that quilt right out of her hand and give it to someone else to finish?"

"Momma," Eudora heard Allison say, "there's nobody can quilt like her. Those tiny stitches. So perfect. So straight."

Eudora smiled. Enjoying herself for the first time since she got stuck in this confounded hospital bed. And then it happened. Her peace was ruined. Bernice Holloway walked in the door.

Eudora picked up her bowl of pees and threw it toward her neighbor. They showered down on Bernice like confetti on New Year's. The bowl bouncing off her arm and clattering to the floor.

"You belong in the psych ward. That's where they outta put you," Bernice said brushing pees out of her hair and clothes. "But it's gonna take more than a bowl full of pees to get rid of me. I can tell you that for sure. I'm spending the night. Getting a cot rolled in."

"Fiddle-faddle. You snoopy old busy body. Now go on outta here and leave me alone. I don't need you in here stinking up my air," Eudora said.

"You're the busy body. You can't get rid of me just cause you say so. I said I'm spending the night, and I'm spending the night. You need someone to take care of you. Besides, hurricane's coming and they're sending everyone to shelters anyway. "

"Go to a shelter then. Don't stay here and pollute my air."

"You know what I like about you?" Bernice asked.

Eudora looked over at her.

"Nothing."

"Ditto," Eudora snipped. "Now git."

Bernice bent over and started picking up the pees that had pooled at Eudora's bedside. She tossed them in the garbage, brushed her hands together, and put them on her hips. "Now you listen here Miss Eudora. For nigh on decades I have put up with your bad mood. Now I just as soon let you rot, but I'm a good Christian woman even if you aren't. I'm also a good citizen, and I'll be tarred and feathered if I'm gonna let anything happen to you. Now do you want me to smuggle Betty Grable in or not? I got her out in the car."

The Bayou Press

# Fried Mullet Throwdown Huge Success

Thanks for coming down ya'll. The Twelfth Annual Fried Mullet Throwdown was about as awesome as drinking orange soda packed with peanuts. The winner Beau Wade got a good old crisp on. Salty, crispy, and delicious. Thanks Beau for the best fried mullet yet!

## Eudora's Tips and Tricks
## For Quilter's Daily

### #71

Okay, you hand quilting purists like me, listen up. Ever have trouble pulling a needle through several thicknesses of fabric? Cut a section off the rubber ring you use to seal your jam jars and keep that next to you while you stitch. If things get tough, pick up the rubber, pinch the needle with it, and pull right through. As always...

Happy Quilting!

# Bernice's Quick Recipes
## for Busy Quilters

### #3

Well ladies, I know you're gonna think I'm crazy. I know I promised you short, quick recipes, but hear me out. Now the woman who shall not be named mentioned jelly jar rubbers in her little tips and tricks which set me to thinking – maybe some of ya'll would like to make some jellies. Granted, they aren't the quickest thing ever, but if you make a bunch at once, then it is an easy snack from there on out when you're up against a quilting deadline, right? So here goes:

## Apple Jelly

1 pound of apples
pinch of cinnamon
cup of sugar
tablespoon or so of pectin

Wash the apples, peel 'em, core 'em, and chop 'em up. Put about an inch of water in a pot, then cook 'em on high until they're soft. Strain the apples through cheesecloth in a colander. In a small bowl, mix the pectin and some of the sugar. Put the strained apples back in a pot on the stove. Mix in that sugar-pectin mix and bring it to a boil. Add in the rest of the sugar. Pour the jelly in jelly jars. (Make sure you boil everything real good first.) Slap on the jar jellies and the ring. Get jar tongs and dunk the whole thing in boiling water one last time to make sure all those nasty germs are dead. Then they're ready to store in your pantry. They should keep for about a year.

Have You Some Good Eatin'!

# Eleven

"Liar," Eudora screeched. "You don't have a car."

"I didn't say my, my car. The Royce boy dropped me off. He's waiting and he's got Betty Grable. Do you want me to sneak her in or not?"

"I don't care what you do."

"And I brought the quilt."

"What?" Eudora roared. "You touched the quilt? You moved the quilt? Have you completely lost your mind?"

"You're on deadline," Bernice said.

"I would thank you to put my cat and my quilt back where you found them."

"Why can't you just say thank you?" Bernice asked.

"You wouldn't like to hear what I have to say."

"You need your cat. You need to work on the quilt. Who knows how long you'll be in here."

"Don't leave a mess in my house either. I don't want my house looking like that muck shack you live in."

"I'll go get the cat and the quilt and I'll be right back."

Eudora whipped the blanket back and slammed her bare feet down on the cold linoleum.

"You'll do no such thing," she growled. "You've done damage enough already."

"Get back in bed. You'll catch your death," Bernice demanded.

But Eudora marched to the door.

"I can see your hiney. You gonna go out with your hiney showing?" Bernice asked.

Eudora snatched the rear of her gown shut and reached for the door.

"The hurricane's coming," Bernice entreated.

But Eudora opened the door and charged down the hall.

Bernice stuck her head out in the hallway.

"You'll be safer here. On the fourth floor. It's a cinder block building."

But Eudora ignored her neighbor and headed for the elevator.

"This hurricane's headed for Shreveport. You don't know what you're talking about," Eudora shouted toward the ceiling.

Bernice just stood in the middle of the hallway, hands on her hips, shaking her head.

The car pulled up in front of her home and Eudora and Betty Grable hopped out. Eudora with the quilt over her arm.

The air sat very still. The sky hummed clearest blue. The neighborhood quiet. No bikes in the street, casual cars, pedestrians. Everyone had fled north or east to avoid the storm. Eudora just chuckled. If Camille didn't get her, nothing would. Fools and cowards every one.

The Royce boy leaned his head out of his pickup.

"Now Miss Eudora, you know I'd like nothing more than to drive you up north. You can stay with big mama."

"I could never impose."

"You wouldn't be an imposition. But if you feel that way, I could drop you at the Red Cross. They've got a shelter set up in Jackson."

"They won't take pets."

"I can see you've got your mind made up. Good luck to you."

"Thank you son," Eudora said, looking him in the eyes for the first time. There she noticed a navy blue ring around a grayer inner iris. Off set with the blackish-brown hair swirling like puffs of smoke. His nose and forehead pink with the sunburn of two-a-days. But those eyes. That navy blue ring around his iris. Just like Frank. Why did every corner have to remind her of Frank? I Sewanee.

The Bay Press Special Sunday Series

## Cajun Folk Tales

As ya'll well know, Cajun culture been seepin' through our bayous since the 1700s. So we thought it might be fun to print some of the tales we've heard over the years, seeing as Louisiana and Mississippi share a lot of the same history. This one's been circulatin' for ages. Hope you folks enjoy.

## The Old Hip Boots

## Retold by Cairo

A pretty young missy, as pretty as sun settin' on them bayou waters married a hunter-fisherman. He loved her and she loved him. They were as happy as a ladybug on a daisy.

One day, the husband went a-fishin' back in them bayou waters and next thing you know another fisher found him dead and floatin' face down.

Heartbroken was the young missy. Here she was nigh on twenty and she already a widow.

Soon another young fellow in town starting lookin' at her and sniffin' around. Before you slap a swatter on a housefly, they married. And he a hunter-fisher too.

One day, the husband wade on back through those marshy bayous to catch him some alligator for supper. He didn't come home that night and the widow-now-wife she get all worried again. She don't like be lonesome and widowed again. But sure enough another hunter found him dead sitting up in his tree stand dead as grass in drought.

Now the other young men in town start getting suspicious and avoid her house. The women gossip and kids take a wide berth. If a young man did get up the courage to visit her, she was darn sure pretty enough, lagniappe for sure, his family would warn him away say she sure enough killed her first husband and her second and did he wanna be her third.

Then a Yankee come on down from way up north, probably Natchez. Sure far enough north, for sure. He a drummer, selling goods town to town, no hunting and fishing for him. He also don't have family to tell him no way. But he hear the stories sure. Drummers supposed to be wise you know from all they travels. So he study the deaths of these husbands cause he wanna marry this widow sure enough.

In the closet, he finds some hip boots they each wore to go out hunting and fishing. He studies them close up and find a rattlesnake fang in the heel. He know now the widow don't kill them men. They poisoned by the fang, so he burn the boots and live happily ever after with that pretty young missy still only nigh on twenty-three.

Now they dance the fais-do-do to zydeco singing "laissez les bon temps roulez" all the way.


Moral: Beware of snakes in them there bayous.

The Bay Press

## Army Cpl. Forrest Owen Buried in Biloxi

We hold our breath and pray this day never comes when we send our young soldiers to war. But this time the worst has come true. Our own Forrest was buried at First Baptist last Thursday after being killed by enemy fire over there in the Middle East desert somewheres.

Friends and family attended the service as well as our U.S. rep. Jordan Jones.

Highlights include when Forrest's aunt, Aida Reed, got up and read John 15:13, "No greater love has any man than this, that he lay down his life for his friends."

As you might imagine, his parents are devastated. Please bring casseroles to Tom and Donna when you can. Tom's favorite is lasagna.

Forrest's fiancé Melissa Walker took to her parent's bed when she heard the news and hasn't been seen since. I'm sure the Walker's could use some pie. Melissa always did favor rhubarb.

We reprinted the picture from before their senior prom below. Poor Forrest is trying to pin the corsage on Melissa under Tom's watchful eye.

The Bay Press

## Comedy Corner

"Things you won't ever hear a Southerner say"

Here's this week's winners (and the politically correct police can please stop writing in about stereotypes, thank you, this is all in fun, so loosen up):

1. Don't do that. Fireworks are illegal.
2. Ewww, fried mullet. Mullet are bottom feeders.
3. No cold beer for me, please. It's fattening.
4. Football is on? Actually, I'm a soccer fan.
5. Pink flamingoes in the front yard? How tacky!

# Twelve

Cajun spice in a shrimp boil, that's what Eudora smells when she walks in her front door.

"Frank!" Eudora shouts.

"What?" he says, jutting his head into the front room.

Eudora drags the sewing and scrap boxes to the dining table.

"I have to sew all night. We can't use the table for food."

"You have to eat, don't you?" Frank asks, the clang of pots echoing from the kitchen.

"What do I say about spice in the house when I'm sewing?" Eudora asks.

"Fine. I'll just take dinner next door. I'm sure Bernice would like some."

"You're trying to make me jealous? Go ahead."

"I think I will."

"If you think you can wade through all the junk," Eudora says.

"I can find my way through mashed potatoes eight feet deep."

"Who ever heard of mashed potatoes eight feet deep? That doesn't even make sense."

"What do you care? I'm bringing boiled shrimp platters to Bernice's."

"She's not even home, you bozo."

"I should have known."

"What's that supposed to mean?"

"You wouldn't send me over unless she wasn't there."

"What?"

"You heard me."

"You can start speaking English any time."

"You're rude."

"I have a deadline. Now scat. I don't have time for this nonsense."

"Amen."

Eudora hears a clanging and slamming and knows Frank has left out the back door. She bends toward her quilt, puts on her glasses, and picks up her needle.

She matched the blue corduroy to the seam and began her meticulous stitches. She was entering her quilt in the Innovators category where she knew the judges would appreciate an unconventional fabric choice – especially, as in this case, when a fabric like corduroy was being used to represent water.

She sat there for hours, for days, these days piled upon her years, stitching by hand, tiny stitch after tiny stitch. Despite her considerable age and questionable eyesight, she hunched over the quilt with a hand as steady as the highest priced surgeon in New Orleans.

Her concentration so intense she didn't even notice that Betty Grable had chased a mouse through the front room or that Bernice had stuck her head in to check on her. But she did notice that a plate of sausage balls appeared on her kitchen counter.

"I don't like sausage balls!" Eudora shouted at the ceiling.

"You'll like mine," she heard from across the yard.

Eudora chuckled and shook her head. She hunched over her needlework and kept her pace adding a strip of velvet here, brocade there. A cornucopia of colors and textures. A quilt unlike any other. As she worked, the needle moving in and out of the fabric, she drifted into a kind of trance. Hours melted away as she focused on the task at hand.

Toward midnight, she hears Frank call to her from the bedroom.

"Eudora, you coming to bed?"

"Don't bother me while I'm working," she grunts. "I might just have to give you a whooping. As my daddy used to always say, 'A belt serves a greater purpose than just holding up your pants.'"

The Bay Press Special Sunday Series

## Cajun Folk Tales

Ya'll will recognize this one. Old Thibodeaux tells it down at the French Market every Sunday.

## The Old Door

## Retold by Cairo

Boudreaux's momma head to market to sell some collards she grow in the backyard. They poor as potatoes and she try to make ends meet. Before she leave, she make Boudreaux promise to guard the door to their home while she gone.

His momma gone a long time and he start get worried. He wanna go check on her but he know she told him to guard the door. So he take the door off the hinges, load it on his back, and go look for her.

As he trot down the road with the door on his back, he see three robbers come running toward him with a sack of stuff.

Young Boudreaux, he got scared and clumb up in a tree with the door. The robbers stopped under him and started counting the cash in the sack.

"A third for you, a third for you, and a third for me," the leader say.

"And a third for me," Boudreaux shouted from the branches. The robbers got scared and stared up in the tree, but they couldn't see past the leaves and such.

"A third for you, a third for you, and a third for you," the leader say again.

"And a third for me," Boudreaux added and threw the door down on them.

The leader shouted, "The devil's raining doors down on us as punishment."

The three robbers jump up and run away.

Boudreaux hop down out of the tree, load the door on his back, put the cash in the sack, and take it home to his momma. Now maybe they don't be poor as potatoes no more.

When his momma see that money, she so happy she hug his neck and boo-hoo.

Moral: Don't steal, always be doing what momma  says, and the meek shall inherit the earth. Amen.

## Eudora's Tips and Tricks
## For Quilter's Daily

### #75

Now ladies, don't even waste your money on quilter's chalk. Those marks are as hard to get out as the last millimeter of honey in a narrow neck jar. Use underarm deodorant for those lines and keep some old knee highs in your sewing basket. When you're done, rub the marks with the nylons and they come right up. You don't have to bother yourself with washing the quilt to get the chalk out (you know my feeling about washing a competition quilt). As always…

Happy Quilting!

## Bernice's Quick Recipes
## for Busy Quilters

### #4

It's hurricane season, so I know a lot of you folks will head on the road to get away from the storms. Don't be stoppin' at those fast food restaurants when you can bring you some home cookin'.

Here's an easy sandwich that's great to pack up in a picnic basket and eat in the car.

Shrimp Po' Boy

French Bread
Mayo
Dill Pickle Slices
Shredded Lettuce
Tomato Slices
Fried Shrimp
Hot Sauce

Slice the bread, but leave it hinged so all the fixings won't fall out.

Spread mayonnaise. Then sprinkle lettuce, pickles and tomatoes. Top with the Fried Shrimp. Pack some beer, hot sauce, and crunchy kettle chips to go with.

If you want a great fried shrimp recipe, keep reading…

Fried Shrimp

> 3 cups vegetable oil
> 1 cup flour
> ½ cup corn flour
> ½ cup corn meal
> 2 shakes of creole seasoning
> 2 shakes of garlic powder
> 2 shakes of onion powder
> 2 shakes of seasoned salt
> 1 egg
> 1 pound peeled, de-tailed, and de-veined
>   medium Gulf Coast shrimp

Heat the oil in a deep cast iron skillet. Mix the flour and seasonings in a baggie. Beat the egg in a bowl. Mix the corn flour and corn meal in another baggie. Cook the shrimp in batches. Put it in the flour bag, shake it up, dip it in the egg wash, then put it in the corn bag, and shake it up. Drop in oil. Drain by putting it on paper towels stacked on a plate. (Make sure you let the oil get hot again before you drop in the next batch.)

Have you some good eatin'!

Bernice's Quick Recipes
for Busy Quilters

#5

Another great treat to take on the road in the event of a hurricane evacuation is boiled peanuts. Here's how I make 'em:

Boiled Peanuts

2 pounds raw green peanuts
3 quarts of water
Tons of salt

Wash the peanuts and drain them in a colander. Boil the water. Add the peanuts and the salt. Cook on a slow boil for two hours. Add more water and salt as necessary. Once they're soft, turn the heat off and let sit for thirty minutes. Drain.

Have you some good eatin'!

The Bay Press

## Comedy Corner

"Things you won't ever hear a Southerner say."

Here's this week's winners:

1. I don't really care for beef jerky.
2. Pork rinds are gross.
3. No thank you, I'm a vegetarian.
4. Your truck tires are too big.
5. I don't eat fried food. It's not healthy.

## Thirteen

The neighborhood had been abandoned and quiet for some time, but now the quiet was heavier, heavy like a warm, wet washcloth. Eudora paused and looked up from her needlework. No frog. No cricket. No wind. She wondered if she had gone deaf and snapped her fingers to test. But she heard the snap, dry and sharp.

She folded the corner of the quilt over and placed it on the table. Then she pulled her tomato pin cushion out of her sewing box, placed it on the corner, and stabbed her needle into it.

Eudora took her glasses off, stood up, and walked to the front window looking out over Dogwood. She pulled the curtain back and leaned forward to peer out on the dirt road crossing in front of her house. Then the air smelled different. Like the air after a strike of lightning. Was it ionized? Eudora wasn't sure. Next the howl, a moaning but sharper. Now higher, a whistle, like a kettle of water on for tea. Eudora stepped back, but it was too late. The window exploded and crashed in on her, a thousand shards of glass pushing her to the ground. She lay there flat on her back as the wind tore through her front room. She tried to sit up, but the wind knocked her down again. She saw the pillows from her sofa and a few copies of *Quilter's Daily* swirling above her in a mini tornado. She tried to sit up again, but her stomach muscles were no match for the hurricane force winds. The wind knocked her back, slamming her head on the floor. She covered her ears with her hands to dull the pounding sound, like a train thundering through her front room.

Eudora rocked back and forth until she gained enough momentum to roll over on her stomach. The wind started pulling the raindrops into the room and the water stung her like so many mosquito bites. The wind lulled and she pushed herself up on to her hands and knees, crawling to the back room. She got there, turned and closed the door, and stood up with her back against it. She felt pressure. The door bumped behind her like a thief was pushing in, hungry for jewels. Eudora locked the door then walked over and sat on the bed. She took a tissue from the box by the bed and blew her nose. Then she saw it.

There under both doors seeped water. Quickly rising water. Muddy, salty water. It crossed the room quickly. Eudora picked her feet up off the floor as the water crept under the bed. She turned and looked out her bedroom window. The water was already four inches above her sill. She looked back at her bedroom door, the one leading into the house. The water was rising quickly. It already covered three inches of the bottom of the door.

Eudora stood up on her bed and prayed for the water to go down. She especially hoped it would go down before it blew out her bedroom window. She screamed for help but the wind and rain were so loud she couldn't even hear herself. It was loud, as loud as Bernice banging pots in Eudora's ear to wake her up to help rake the pine straw off the roof. *Oh that Bernice.*

But the water didn't go down. It rose on the door from six inches to ten. Eudora turned to look at the window. The water, swirling green and gray, covered two-thirds. In it, she saw a spoon, then an azalea branch, and then a scrap of calico. The dual panic seized Eudora all at once. Betty Grable and the quilt.

Just then, the window exploded sending in a rushing current of water. It knocked Eudora off the bed and twisted her in the whirlpool. Her wrist was slammed against a wall. Her hips pushed up over her head. She flipped again, felt the bed with her foot, and pushed toward the surface. As her head broke through, she saw the roof vibrating, shaking. A corner peeled up, slammed down, shook, and broke away. Eudora knew it was a tornado and soon the whole roof was gone.

She saw branches, boards, metal, and all manner of debris flying overhead. She gulped air and ducked under the water as she felt her walls fall away. A book hit her shoulder and she pushed to the surface for more air. She came up beside a section of roof with chimney, floating. Eudora crawled up and lay spread eagle, face down. She heard a *meow* and turned her head sharply to the right. Betty Grable's head stuck out of the chimney. Her front paws curled around the edge. The cat jumped up and out, crept over to Eudora, and crouched between her head and shoulder. The two stayed low as shards of glass, legs of furniture, tricycles, a football, rakes, all the debris of a neighborhood flew overhead. She couldn't see out of her right eye. She wiped it and looked at her hand. Blood.

The Bay Press

## pennySMART Shelves Bare Naked

Gulf Coasters have cleared the shelves at pennySMART in preparation for the category 5 hurricane hovering offshore. Lumber, canned goods, water bottles, duct tape, hammers, nails, candles, batteries, flashlights, battery operated radios, and generators were all "gone baby gone."

The governor has issued a mandatory evacuation and closed the southbound highways and freeways. All roads are open northbound only.

Don't forget to clean up all debris, branches, lawnchairs, lawn gnomes, and flamingoes etc. If it ain't nailed down or tucked inside, throw it away. Remember, all that stuff becomes a projectile breaking out your neighbors' windows in hurricane force winds. Last garbage pick up tomorrow mornin'. Be sure to head for the highway by two. Power will be shut off at 2:30pm sharp.

Sheriff Tucker asked me to remind you that mandatory evacuation means no one can come help you if you get in trouble. Don't get that stubborn Southern mentality about staying and for goodness gracious sake, do not throw a hurricane party.

# Bernice's Quick Recipes
## for Busy Quilters

## #6

Now I recognize that I'm getting' a little off my track of "quick recipes for busy quilters." But I have it on good authority that more than a handful of ya'll gonna stay on the coast and throw a hurricane party.

I've worked on this for several years and I'm telling you this is hands down the best hurricane recipe South of the Mason-Dixon line.

### Hurricane

6 shots of vodka
6 shots of gin
6 shots of light rum
3 shots of 151 rum
6 shots of amaretto
6 shots of triple sec

2 dashes of grenadine
juice from one squeezed lime
dash of superfine sugar
equal parts grapefruit juice, pineapple juice,
orange juice

Stir in a pitcher and pour over ice.

Serve in: Hurricane Glass
Garnish with: cherry and orange slice on umbrella
Makes: 6 glasses

Have you some good drinkin'!

# Fourteen

Eudora's makeshift raft hit up against another and another. Soon a great debris field spread out in front of her made up of roofs and walls from the houses in her neighborhood. Some the pastels from Peachtree. Others the natural hues of Hargrove. She saw a large chimney, larger than hers, so she stood up, grabbed Betty Grable, and started walking across the debris. A gust of wind in a duet with a wave pushed her sideways. She felt a line across her back and turned to see that the wind was blowing her up against the power lines. This meant she was floating far above the rooftops, twenty feet or so off the ground. She had lived here all her life, but she had never seen a storm surge like this one.

She crouched down, sheltering the cat between her ducked head, curved shoulders, and rounded arms. When the wind calmed, Eudora stood holding the cat and walked across the debris field to the larger chimney she had seen before. As she walked, she got slammed in the hip with a flying branch. Betty Grable clung to her. Eudora hurried behind the chimney, put the cat down, and picked up a barstool to fend off flying debris. She knocked away soda cans, water bottles, and a jump rope. Then a bicycle tire, a large shard of glass, and a broom. Betty Grable pressed up against the chimney wall, her wet fur clumping into jagged spikes.

The water continued to rise, the last leaves of the oak trees disappearing under the swells. A few needles from the top branches of pine trees still twisting in the wind. She smelled the sour smell of death and closed her eyes.

She smelled broccoli, boiled broccoli. Not the fresh smell of the lightly steamed, but the suffocating stench of the over-boiled, no seasoning, no butter. Not unlike the stench in a house suffocating in boiling cabbage cooking all Sunday, or maybe Brussels sprouts. She opened her eyes and continued down the hallway at the Army hospital. They told her he had a traumatic brain injury and had lost his legs. She imagined the bandage on his head, the flat place under the blanket on the bed where his legs should be.

She continued to put one foot in front of the other literally forcing herself, pushing herself down the hallway. Ammonia occasionally cutting in on the smell of boiled broccoli. She looked to her right, a half step behind here, and there was Bernice, walking beside her on this, one of the worst days of this life.

"Help."

Eudora heard the word, light and faint on the wind.

"Help," faint again.

Eudora held on to the chimney and stood up. The wind pushed her back and she struggled to keep her balance. Her short white curls blew in her face. She pushed them back, but the wind growled, insistent.

"Help."

There it was. She heard it again. It was coming from the west. The rain started, like so many sewing needles stabbing into her skin. Eudora tried to open her eyes and look toward the sound, but the rain flew horizontally driving her eyelids instinctively closed.

"Help."

There. She heard it. Behind her now. She bent forward and looked under her right arm, the chimney shielding some of the rain. She saw a figure hanging onto the top branch of a pine tree. It was just a grey lump in the fierce storm, but Eudora could make out appendages woven through pine needles, arms she supposed.

The wind was driving her toward the tree, her and the chimney a sort of sail. Betty Grable hugging the shingles of the roof, now raft. The ocean rising and falling by twenty feet at a time, a vat of molten lead. And just as dangerous.

The Bay Press Special Sunday Series

## Cajun Folk Tales

This is a popular one down at Lil Abe's. Boyd likes to tell it when he's had one to many (if you know what I mean).

## The Mississippi River Captain, Braggadacio

## Retold by Cairo

The Mississippi River was a-stormin' that night. None of the riverboat captains dare be on the river. They gathered in a bar on the riverbank and you could hear 'em say, "The devil is in the Mississippi River this night."

They said ya'll could see the devil in them eddies a-swirlin' against the helms of the riverboats. And they could hear him in the blat of the riverboat horns. And then they could see him in the dim lanterns barely cuttin' through the fog.

"Yes sir," those riverboat captains nodded their heads and agreed, "The devil is sure enough in the river this night." It was no kinda night to be out in a riverboat.

But here was one young captain, Braggadacio. He alone said he could navigate the Mississippi River no matter what the weather, no matter if the devil was in the river or not. The young captain brag that he know the twists and the turns, the snags and the banks of that there Mississippi River so well that rain, nor fog, nor swells could keep him from making his run.

The other captains listened to him a-braggin' away. Then they laughed and told him he would be right back, tail between his legs, if he tried to head on out there. The young captain, Braggadacio, got madder and madder then left abruptly to take the helm of his riverboat.

He push off from the dock to begin his journey. He know the river as well as any captain in that bar and he would show them for sure. Suddenly, the boat ran aground and threw him backward to the deck, but this could not happen. He know the shoreline and the river bottom like he know his own face in the mirror. But it was true. The storm had shifted the river in the night.

The next morning the captains went out to look for their foolish young friend. They found his riverboat sunk and him dead at the helm.

Now they say, on stormy nights, they can still hear the sound of his engine and see his lights yearning to cut the fog as the young captain, Braggadacio, stubborn and arrogant to the end, tries to complete his run.

Moral: Don't go out on the Mississippi River in a big ol' storm. That river bottom's liable to shift on ya.

# Eudora's Tips and Tricks
## For Quilter's Daily

## #76

Now ladies, you know when you buy a comforter at pennySMART how it comes in a large plastic pouch with a zipper? Always save those. When a hurricane's coming and it looks like things might be gettin' more than a little wet, fold up your valuable quilts and store in those waterproof pouches. Put 'em on the top shelf of your closet. It'll keep 'em high and dry. As always…

Happy Quilting!

The Bay Press

# Royce Boy Killed in Deadly Hurricane

I know I don't even need to tell ya'll how much it pains me to write this. I just can't believe it. No how. No way. No sense stallin'. Here it is.

Kenneth L. Royce, Kenny to his friends and family, had packed up his pickup after doing some last minute errands for family and friends. He was plum wore out and decided to take a little nap before heading out on the highway. That's the last his mom heard of him. She, like the rest of us, thought the storm was probably headed northwesterly anyway.

I hardly need to tell you the rest. We all watched the news from Jackson or Meridian, Mobile or Pensacola, wherever we traveled to ride out the storm, as the hurricane took a sudden right and the eye ripped right through the middle of Bay St. Louis.

They didn't hear from him for three days and couldn't get back in because of all the debris and national guard, plus the roads were washed out. But ya'll know that already.

My sorrow runs as deep as that surge was, as deep as the Mississippi River at some places. I just can't believe that little ol' boy is gone. I remember when he was born sixteen years ago. I brought his momma a tiny little circle quilt for the crib. Ya'll know the circles stand for eternal love and bonds. You know, the family.

Funeral services are this Tuesday at the Reines Funeral Home. Then burial out back. Be sure to bring your casseroles to Janey. She's a wreck, that's for sure.

# Fifteen

Eudora watched the figure as it struggled to hold on to the tree against the attacks of wave and wind. Her back pressed against the brick of the chimney, Betty Grable huddled beside her.

The surge pushed her closer to the pine tree. She reached for the figure, but was still too far away. She saw a wave knock one arm lose. Then the arm grasped for a second branch and missed. A huge wave came crashing over the tree and when the water receded Eudora saw no figure at all. She stood and looked in every direction, but all she saw were debris fields like the one she was on, the tops of a few pines, and a vast stretch of ocean.

A second wave came crashing over her bit of roof, knocking Eudora off into the sea. She felt herself sinking into the salt water, a heaviness she couldn't explain. She went limp and felt her body twisted and pulled in the tides. Suddenly, a great rush came up under her, pushing her to the surface. Her head hit the corner of the roof. She grabbed the edge and hoisted herself back on. She crawled around the chimney to look for Betty Grable, but the cat was gone.

Eudora crawled to the chimney and slumped against it, her chin pressed against her chest. Another wave came and washed her back into the surf.

She felt kneaded by the water. Worked through with fingertips, punched, flipped, gathered together, and rolled apart. Massaged by tide, pushed and pulled. She decided not to think, and this is what she didn't think about: she didn't think about their first kiss over a vanilla malt at Parry's or the time she first saw him crossing the street to City Hall; she didn't think about the daisies he brought to the door on their first date or the spicy musk cologne she smelled on his neck at the Joan Crawford movie; she didn't think about the record he used to play over and over – Glenn Miller; she didn't think about the red nail polish she wore on short nails or the fact that he was left handed; she didn't remember his gumbo or his secret barbeque sauce with a dash of bourbon or the bee sting she got at their first picnic when his elbow brushed her breast and he pretended not to notice and she let him; and she didn't think about the smell of freshly mowed grass as they walked hand in hand down the center of Peachtree imagining they lived there or the smell of the first wood burning in chimneys when he held her hand in early October. As she was kneaded and worked and turned by the sea, she refused to think about the first whispered I love you as they watched fireworks on the fourth of July in the town square or the watermelon they ate on the blanket right before, spitting the seeds in a Dixie cup, or the homemade peach ice cream; she didn't remember the crawfish, peeling back the shell or sucking the heads and she didn't think about boiling them in cayenne pepper.

But, as she felt a hand on her neck, pulling her up and over and on to the roof, she did think about this: the dress she wore the day he left. She had sewn it herself. It was navy blue cotton with white polka dots and white piping on the sleeves and collar. She had modified it from a Butterick pattern. Shortening the skirt and sleeves. Tapering it more severely at the waist. The buttonholes, she remembered, had been particularly difficult. She had cut them too small, had to rip out the stitching, cut them larger, and refinish them. Of course, the easier option would have been to go to pennySMART and buy smaller buttons, but he had been with her to pick out the first set. In fact, he had found them. They were *his* favorite. One inch in diameter. Flat and opalescent. Eudora wanted to make buttonholes for those exact buttons. The sleeves stopped just six inches below her shoulder blade. They were cuffed up two inches and piped in white. The piping slipped into the stitching with no trouble at all. Although it was a little more difficult to get it to bend around the notched collar. Bernice had loaned her the pearls she had gotten as a wedding present from her husband. A ten millimeter strand, sixteen inches. Of course, they weren't real pearls. But they looked real and that's all that mattered. Eudora had two buttons left over. She broke off the back and glued clips she found in the craft section of pennySMART on the back. She wore these as earrings. They matched the buttons on her dress and the opalescence blended well with the pearls. Her hat was white and short brimmed, curved up sharply a good four inches all around. And her gloves were the standard white issue of pennySmart. Nothing special there. Her handbag, well that was another matter. Her handbag she had found at the thrift store and it was real leather. A clutch with a bright gold snap. She was very proud of that handbag. She never could have afforded it new. It was a real Nicole Matly. Why she'd have to go to the most exclusive department store in Atlanta for something like that. There were two scratches on the bottom of the purse, but she dabbed white shoe polish on them and they hardly even showed.

Eudora caught her breath, lying there on her little square of roofing. She looked up to see a figure blacked out by the sun behind her. As storm clouds moved back over the light, she could see her rescuer: Bernice Holloway, of all people.

"Oh great," Eudora moaned. "You'll never let me forget this."

"That's a fine kettle of fish," Bernice retorted. "Here I am sacrificing my own well-being for a dramatic rescue in the Gulf of Mexico during a category five hurricane and this is the thanks I get."

"Have you seen Betty Grable?"

"You're welcome for saving your life."

Suddenly, a wave came up over the raft and swallowed Bernice. For a split second, Eudora was certain that God had finally answered her prayers. Here was her moment. The human she had most despised in life had been swept overboard by what may reasonably be called the hand of God.

Eudora rolled on her side and watched Bernice flail in the churning water, water gray and angry like a shark. Eudora imagined the peace and quiet she would enjoy if she just let Bernice sink under the waves. Eudora also smiled at the justice of this ending. After Bernice had rubbed her wedding in Eudora's face. This was a fitting farewell to such hateful behavior. Eudora began to giggle as she thought of the first thing she would do after the hurricane, with Bernice gone: she would cut down that irritating willow tree. Just think, no more fronds littering her yard. What joy. What justice. What peace on earth.

Eudora lay on her side and looked out over the sea rising and falling. Her raft bumped against the branches of an oak tree as she saw a wave crash over Bernice and watched her hands claw for the surface. Then a flash of color caught Eudora's eye. She turned to see her championship quilt tangled in one of the tree's branches. She reached for the quilt, the wind yanked it away. She looked toward Bernice, she didn't see anything, then two fingers. She looked back to the quilt straining, pulled by the wind. If Eudora stretched, she could just get it before the wind ripped it away forever. She looked back in Bernice's direction, she saw her hand reach up, her face break the surface of the water to gasp for air. Eudora groaned and reached her arm out to grasp the desperate fingers of the left hand as the wind ripped the quilt from the branches and whipped it out of sight.

Bernice grasped her tightly as Eudora pulled her back on the raft.

Bernice lay splayed, akimbo, on her stomach, sputtering and coughing salt water up from her lungs. She wheezed and hacked.

"Now we're even," she finally sputtered.

"Forget about it," Eudora replied.

"I know you wanted to let me drown."

"Don't be ridiculous."

"You're the ridiculous one. Cleaning all the time. Raking lines into your yard."

"It's better than living with gum stuck under coffee tables. Candy wrappers in your bedside table drawers. Coffee grounds on the floor of your kitchen."

"I'm gonna do a spring cleaning."

"Spring? You haven't cleaned in twenty years."

"At least I've had a life in the past twenty years."

"You have not. *I've* had a life."

"Runner up in quilt contests, maybe winning one or two here and there or honorable mention is not a life."

"Lame recipes in a quilter's magazine is a life?"

"My recipes are not lame."

"Sometimes they're not even recipes. They're drunk suggestions."

"Everyone needs a hurricane recipe. I was trying to be topical. You know darn well there were hurricane parties up and down this coast."

"I wish you'd get your own group of friends. You poached your husband off my fiancé. You poached your column off mine. And cut down that willow tree. I'm tired of cleaning up after you all my life."

"At least I'm not Miss Priss. You scrub your doormat. You leave your shoes at the front door. You steam your glasses. You can't bring flowers in because they're dirty. And you're afraid they might shed some leaves on your precious floor. Or worse yet, bring in insects. Horrors. Which incidentally I have watched you scrub your front porch with bleach twice a week for decades. Why don't you live a little? Learn to let go? Embrace the chaos in the universe and give it a big old smooch."

Bernice kissed Eudora's cheek.

Eudora screamed and pushed Bernice away, but Bernice couldn't hear what she said. The hurricane winds were rising again, and the two women pressed themselves flat against the roofing, clinging to the corners.

Eudora realized she would have to wait until later to give Bernice her comeuppance. So she settled down on her stomach and turned her face to the side, her right ear resting on the shingles. She closed her eyes and suddenly she wasn't sure she would have the opportunity to yell at Bernice after all. The swells rose and fell ten, maybe twenty feet. The wind tore at her hair and ripped her clothes to tatters. But with her right ear pressed to the shingles she almost felt like she could hear voices, voices from inside her house, inside her past.

"Is this really the time to polish all the wood in your front room?" she hears him ask.

Eudora pours orange oil on one of his old t-shirts and rubs the wooden arms on the couch.

"What's wrong with now?" she asks.

"We're supposed to be at Bernice's birthday party," he answers.

"I can't stand to come home to a dirty house. You go on ahead."

"I don't want to go without you," he says. "I'm only going because you asked me to. Heck, I didn't want to go in the first place."

"Then what's the rush?' she asks. "Take a seat." She motions to the couch.

He sighs, crosses to the couch, and sits down.

"Eudora," he starts.

She pours more oil into the t-shirt and rubs it into the coffee table.

"Yes," she says, not bothering to look up from her task.

"Did it ever occur to you that you keep yourself busy cleaning and such because you're trying to avoid something?"

"Avoid something? What would I want to avoid? Fiddle-faddle. You say the craziest things.

Why, I couldn't be happier. I'm not avoiding anything, anything at all."

"It's just that you seem to clean when you're upset or maybe you don't want to think about something or do something," he adds. "Do you wanna talk about your daddy?"

Eudora crosses to the dining chairs, pours more oil in the rag, and begins rubbing down the spokes in the back.

"I appreciate your concern. I surely do. But there's nothing wrong with keeping a clean house. 'Cleanliness is next to Godliness,' the preacher always says."

"You never talk about your daddy. Do you want to talk about him now? It couldn't have been easy seeing him, without legs I mean," he says.

Eudora crosses to the kitchen. She throws away the rag, tucks the oil up under the sink, and washes her hands.

"Don't be ridiculous. We've got a birthday party to get to. There's no time for that nonsense."

And with that, she picks up her handbag, hooks it on her arm, juts her chin up high, and walks out the back screen door. Dropping it to a heavy clatter behind her.

The Bay Press

Comedy Corner

"Things you won't ever hear a Southerner say."

Here's this week's winners:

1. A hurricane's coming? Then I guess I *won't* go to the liquor store.
2. A hurricane's coming? Cancel the party.
3. Turn off the football game. We need to prepare for the hurricane.
4. I hate the taste of beer.
5. Chewing tobacco causes cancer.

## Eudora's Tips and Tricks
## For Quilter's Daily

### #77

Now ladies, as ya'll husbands are bringin' home all that plywood to batten up the hatches for the incoming hurricane, get them to build you a quick quilt stand with the leftovers. Heck, they already have the saws, nails, and hammers out. Nothing's more decorative than a hand sewn quilt. A nice quilt stand allows you to display it in your bedroom or even in the living room. As always…

Happy Quilting!

## Sixteen

As quickly as the water had risen, it began to retreat. The wind slowed to short gusts while the rain stopped altogether. Bands of clouds striped across the sky with bars of summer blue now insistent between them. Eudora stretched out on the raft, looking up, and thought how strange it was to see no seagull, no butterfly, no dragonfly, no mosquito, nothing in the air.

When the water got shallow enough to reveal the top of some recognizable azalea bushes from up the coast, Eudora and Bernice pushed themselves off the roofing and waded northeast. Boats were lodged between trees. People's clothes strung up through branches. Bay St. Louis looked like it had been in a blender for six hours or maybe like it had been the victim of an atomic bomb.

It was slow going. The retreating water tugged at their ankles, threatening to pull them out to sea. But the two women were determined and grabbed on to tree trunks, phone poles, and branches when the force got to be too much – at times their bodies drifting out parallel to the ground.

More distressing was the migration of debris southward with the tide. Glass, lumber, tools, furniture, all threatened to cut and batter Eudora and Bernice while they trudged on. Some objects succeeded.

As they moved inland, Eudora noticed that the water near the mouth of a bayou was rushing more quickly than the surrounding waters. She turned to warn Bernice away from the flow when she saw her neighbor lose her footing and go under, slipping toward the rushing waters. Eudora grabbed a branch with her right hand then grabbed Bernice's departing ankle with the other and pulled her in. Bernice grabbed Eudora's branch, spit out a mouthful of saltwater, and wiped her eyes.

"Two-one," Bernice said.

"Don't remind me," Eudora sighed.

Eudora again took off, trudging northward and eastward. Bernice trailing behind her. The water thinner and thinner until their feet were sticking in the thinnest layer of bayou mud, which covered everything.

Then it happened. Eudora heard the creak of wood. She turned to see Bernice lagging behind. An instant later, Eudora's eye caught the movement of a pine tree falling. She rushed forward, but this time she was too late. The pine tree crushed Bernice underneath its trunk. Splitting her through the middle.

Eudora felt the wind rush out of her lungs. She stood frozen, blinking at what she was seeing. This couldn't be the way this story ends.

Eudora walked toward Bernice and fell to her knees in the mud. She bent over and wrapped her arms around Bernice's shoulders. Hugging her tightly. Forehead to forehead. Until Bernice grew stiff and cold.

Eudora would never know how long this was, but when she would reflect on it in the years that followed, she thought she must have stayed with Bernice for several hours.

As she stood to leave, Eudora paused and turned back to Bernice. "So death is spectacles," she said. "You can't see clearly til you put it on." Eudora paused. She kicked the ground, looked up and examined the sky. Then she turned back to her friend. "I hated you. But I guess I loved you too."

Slowly, numbly, with nothing left to say or do, Eudora walked away in search of the remnants of her neighborhood.

She had trouble finding it with nary a landmark left. But when she finally did, she could not believe what she saw. Where the houses on Peachtree stood, only a few trees. Where the house on Hargrove stood, trees. She walked down Dogwood. There wasn't a wall left standing.

She wandered toward where she thought her house must have been. She believed she found it and stepped onto the foundation and surveyed her property. Then she noticed it. And began to laugh.

Soon her laugh turned to tears until she descended into the hysterics of the insane: the willow tree was gone, uprooted and washed away by the storm. Now nothing more than a shallow puddle of mud.

Eudora wiped her face, sniffed, and blinked. She rested on her foundation, spread eagle, and closed her eyes. Suddenly she heard it. A tiny meow. She opened her eyes to see Betty Grable jump from the lowest branch on a nearby oak tree and run toward her. Eudora felt her heart lurch. She sat up, clutched Betty Grable to her chest, and scratched her behind the ears. Joy, joy, one ounce of joy. One small blessing in a world of ruin.

Eudora caught sight of something shining in the sun. She put the cat down, stood up, walked to it, brushed off the dirt and leaves, and picked it up. It was the plastic bag she had stored the quilt in. Tucking it ever-so-carefully into the top of the closet. Empty. Except for two small scraps of material inside. She looked around. She saw two more swatches in the front yard. She crossed to pick them up, shake them off, and put them in the bag. Then she found another plastered to a tree trunk. Another stuck up under a floor mat. When she moved the floor mat, she also saw her rake buried in the mud. She picked it up, set the plastic bag on the foundation, walked to where she guessed the dirt road used to be, placed the rake, and pulled it back toward her slab. She came across an apron. She picked it up, dusted it off, and put it on. Betty Grable sat and watched, waving her tail in the summer sun.

When Eudora was done with the first pass, she walked back to the road, matched her placement next to the first mark, and pulled her rake toward her slab again. She continued this process until she had made perfect parallel lines running across her yard. Sometimes debris stood in her way. Eudora picked it up and threw it aside, refusing to let any obstacle alter her lines, unless it was a swatch from her quilt, of course, then she picked it up and slipped it into her apron pocket.

Up to the road, back to the slab, Eudora pulled her rake, occasionally finding a piece of her quilt, picking it up, tucking it in her apron pocket, taking special care all the while to make sure each line and every pass was perfectly even and perfectly straight.

www.ingramcontent.com/pod-product-compliance
Lightning Source LLC
Chambersburg PA
CBHW031259060726
47590CB00003B/971